D0566755

Over the Underworld

Also by Adam Shaughnessy

The Unbelievable FIB 1: The Trickster's Tale

Over the Underworld

by

ADAM SHAUGHNESSY

Algonquin Young Readers 2016

Over the Underworld

CHAPTER 1

THE OLD MAN SAT IN HIS CHAIR AND WATCHED THE FIRE WITH HIS ONE GOOD eye. Two ravens perched nearby, Thought and Memory. He ignored them the way one ignores familiar companions or unwanted guests.

Sometimes he wondered which they were.

As he gazed into the fire before him, he imagined he could see images of gods, giants, and mortals in the dancing flames. They acted out the events of their lives like performers in a show, each playing her or his role.

Now events were occurring that forced him to think about the performance's conclusion.

Sitting there, alone, the old man thought about the days to come.

He thought about the future.

So far, it was going just the way he remembered it.

"MISTER FOX IS A JERK!"

ABE looked around to see if anybody was close enough to have heard Pru's shout. Fortunately, he and Pru stood in a remote section of Middleton Cemetery. The only bodies nearby lay six feet under the ground and probably weren't very interested in Pru's frustration with their former mentor. They stayed quiet.

ABE did, too.

He'd learned that there were two things you didn't talk to Pru about when she was in this kind of mood: One, Mister Fox. Two, everything else.

It was best to just let her work through things on her own.

"He said we'd see him again," Pru complained.

"Well, *technically*, he said it was true we wouldn't see him." The words were out before ABE could stop them. So much for staying quiet.

Pru put her hands on her hips. "You know, ABE, one of these days I'm going to teach you that honesty isn't *always* the best policy."

"Sorry."

"It's okay," Pru said, letting her arms fall to her sides. She sat down on a tree stump and flashed ABE a smile. "It's not you I'm mad at. Not really. Seriously, though. Didn't you think we'd see him again?"

"Yeah, I did. I mean, especially since you thought we would. You always understood him better than I did. Well, except for the time you thought he was Loki and tried to set fire to his house . . ."

"Not helping, ABE. Don't make me change my mind about not being mad at you."

"Right."

Pru sighed. "It's been almost a year."

"Almost," ABE agreed. Mister Fox had arrived in Middleton in his magical Henhouse, headquarters of the Fantasy Investigation Bureau—or, as Mister Fox called it, the Unbelievable FIB—in October of the year before. He'd come to investigate an invasion of gods and giants from Norse mythology.

That's what Mister Fox did. He investigated mysteries that involved magic and myth. But he didn't do it alone. He couldn't. He needed the help of kids. They had a talent for seeing magic where others couldn't. So Mister Fox had recruited ABE and Pru to become Fibbers, junior members of his detective agency. Together, they'd vanquished giants and foiled the attempts of Loki, the Norse trickster, to recover a magical artifact called the Eye of Odin.

But that had all happened last year. Now it was the end of August and school was about to start. Pru and ABE had spent the better part of a year waiting for Mister Fox's return, hiking the wooded trails around Middleton at least once a week. Pru called it patrolling and insisted they do it just to be on the safe side. Their patrols almost always ended in the cemetery, where they could check to see if the Henhouse had returned.

It never had.

Neither had Ratatosk the Insult Squirrel. That's what Pru called him, anyway. Really, Ratatosk was the messenger of the Norse gods. But since so many of the messages he carried were insults, he had developed a rather . . . unique . . . way of speaking to people. Despite that, Ratatosk had become their friend, and ABE missed his company as much as Pru did.

In fact, all the Mythics (Mister Fox's term for beings from Worlds of Myth) who had been in Middleton had left after their battle over the Eye. Even the town patriarch, Old Man Grimnir, who was really Odin in disguise, had left. According to the people who ran the museum wing of his mansion, he'd "gone traveling." No one knew when he'd be back.

"Mister Fox could still show up," ABE said, slipping his looking glass, a gift from the detective, back into his belt.

The looking glass resembled a normal magnifying glass. It had a wooden handle with a brass raven's head at its base and a brass frame around the glass itself. But the device was anything but normal. One side of the glass was actually a mirror that had the power to banish Mythics back to their own world. The other side functioned like a regular magnifying glass, except it could also identify and track Mythics that appeared on Earth.

"I know he *could* still show up. But will he?" Pru glanced at ABE out of the corner of her eye. "I still think we should try my idea to catch his attention in case the Henhouse goes by overhead."

"Pru . . . I figured it out. It would take about fifty-two fallen trees to spell out *MISTER FOX, COME BACK*. And that's assuming all the logs were the same size. I'm not sure we could cut down that many trees. I definitely don't think we should be setting dozens of dead trees on fire."

"Fine." Pru stuck her tongue out. "I'll come up with a new plan."

Pru stood up on the tree stump and pulled her own

looking glass from her messenger bag. It looked a lot like ABE's, only it had a squirrel's head at the base of its handle. She held the glass to her eye and spun in a slow circle. When she'd completed one rotation, she sighed again and slipped her glass back into her bag.

"What if this is it, ABE? What if he doesn't come back and this is it? Just this . . . every day, forever?"

ABE didn't know what to say. A part of him did want to see Mister Fox again. Another part of him wasn't sure. He still had nightmares about when Loki and his chief frost giant, Gristling, had abducted him and taken him to Asgard, the world of the Norse gods.

Silence filled the space between them as the late afternoon sun warmed their skin. Finally, Pru glanced at her watch. "I guess we should be getting back. Tonight's the open house. I can't believe it's time to go back to school already."

"Yeah," ABE agreed. He found himself thinking of fresh school supplies and crisp new textbooks with spines that crackled when you opened them for the first time.

"What do you look so happy about?" Pru asked, eying him suspiciously.

"Me? Oh, nothing." Pru was coming out of her mood about Mister Fox. ABE didn't want to push her buttons by admitting that he was actually excited about the start of a new school year.

"I was just looking at the bright side of school starting," he said instead.

"Which is?"

"Well, we may have to go back to school. But at least you—*we*—won't have to see Mrs. Edleman anymore."

CHAPTER 3

AS HE AND HIS DAD DROVE TO THE SCHOOL THAT NIGHT, ABE WONDERED IF HE had been too optimistic earlier.

It was true that, as seventh graders, he and Pru wouldn't be in Mrs. Edleman's class—or Cell Block E, as Pru called it—anymore. Unfortunately, Middleton was so small that the junior high school was just an addition to the elementary school. It didn't even have its own entrance. So while he and Pru would no longer have to endure Mrs. Edleman's tyrannical approach to public education, they were still likely to see their former teacher every once in a while.

"So," his dad said, "I bet you're disappointed about school starting, huh?"

"Me? Oh . . . yeah." ABE folded up the class schedule he'd been studying and stuffed it in his pocket.

"Right? I know I always hated the end of summer vacation when I was a kid. No more pickup games of Wiffle ball or touch football . . ."

ABE fiddled with his seat belt as his dad's voice trailed off. He tried to think of something he and his dad had in common that they could talk about to fill the sudden quiet. He was still thinking when they pulled into the school's parking lot.

"Well, here we are," his dad said. "And look, there's Pru and her mom."

"ABE, over here!" Pru said, waving, as he and his dad got out of the car. "Hey, Mr. Evans. Catch the game last night?"

"Sure did, sport!"

ABE walked around the back of the car and greeted Pru's mom. "Hi, Mrs. Potts."

"Hi, ABE." She ruffled his hair. She kind of had a fascination with his curly hair. He didn't mind. "Hi, Gavin. No Maddie tonight?"

"Working, unfortunately."

"That's too bad. Well, shall we head inside?" Pru's mom said. "Ready for a new year, Pru?"

"If I say no can I have another month of summer vacation?"

"Nice try, kiddo."

They joined the flow of people walking from the parking lot to the school buildings. The first fallen leaves of the season blew across the pavement in front of them as they approached the entrance.

"What room are we looking for?" Pru's mom asked as they stepped inside.

"Thirteen," Pru answered. "I can't believe our homeroom is number thirteen. Like that's not an omen."

"There are no such things as omens," Pru's mother said. "Don't read anything into a room number. There's no predicting the future."

Pru looked back at ABE and raised her eyebrows dramatically. He hid a grin.

"Looks like this is us," ABE's dad said when they found the right room.

ABE let Pru, her mom, and his dad go in first. He followed them but stopped short just inside the doorway, surprised by the appearance of their new homeroom.

Mrs. Edleman's classroom had been set up with neat rows of desks all facing the front of the room. The walls had been covered with rules.

The desks in this new classroom had been clustered together into makeshift tables with four or five chairs around each. Posters of book covers and pictures of authors lined the walls. ABE beamed when he saw his favorite book, *The Phantom Tollbooth*, among them.

He pulled out his folded schedule. It said what his classes were, and when. It also listed his teachers. He hadn't paid too much attention to his teachers at first—he hadn't recognized any of their names. Now he looked more closely and saw that he had the same teacher for homeroom and language arts, Mr. Jeffries.

"Hey. Who's that?" Pru asked as the four of them settled into seats around a table near the back and a young man with neatly trimmed stubble stepped to the front of the room.

"The adult standing at the front of your homeroom?" Pru's mother asked. "Well, if I was going to go out on a limb, I would guess that's your homeroom teacher. Said the mother to her would-be-detective daughter."

"Funny, mom. Seriously, though. You think? But he's wearing sneakers. Do teachers wear sneakers? Do they even own them? Weird. Imagine Mrs. Edleman in sneakers." Pru shivered in her seat. "Ouch. I think I just broke my brain."

"Shush," her mom said, giving Pru a playful nudge with her elbow. "You'll get me in trouble. There's no talking in class."

ABE smiled. Pru had said she and her mom hadn't always gotten along so well. But they seemed to have a great relationship from what ABE had seen over the past year. He glanced at his dad, who directed a glassy-eyed stare to the front of the room.

"Hi, everyone, and welcome to Middleton Junior High School," the man with the stubble and sneakers said. He gestured to a poster on the wall beside the whiteboard. "One of my favorite poets, Jean Inglelow, once wrote:

Children, ay, forsooth,
They bring their own love with them when they come,
But if they come not there is peace and rest . . .

"Since you've all been good enough to show up tonight, I suppose I can say good-bye to peace and rest."

Chuckles and snorts of laughter filled the room. ABE was surprised that some of the laughter came from Pru.

Not everyone was amused, though. A boy at the table next to theirs whispered to his friend, "*Forsooth*? Who says that? What does it even mean?"

"Actually," ABE said, turning in his seat, "*sooth* is another word for *truth*, so *forsooth* basically means 'in truth.' It's an old English word and—"

Beside him, Pru groaned. ABE turned back to look at her and saw his dad studying the table, red-faced.

"I did the whole ABE-the-walking-dictionary thing again, didn't I?" he whispered to Pru. She nodded. ABE heard snorts of laughter from the table next to theirs. He sank into his chair as his teacher continued speaking.

"I'm kidding, of course. I'm thrilled to see everyone here tonight. I'm Mr. Jeffries. Everyone who's too young to drive a car, I'm going to be your homeroom teacher and your language arts teacher. For everyone else in the room, I'm one of the people your child will likely be complaining about for the next nine months or so. Sorry for that."

More laughter.

"Careful, kiddo," Pru's mother said, leaning in to whisper to Pru. "Someone might actually think you're enjoying yourself at school."

Mr. Jeffries kept them a little longer. He explained the school's website and gave out his e-mail address. Then he invited all the students (and their families) to walk around and meet the rest of their teachers in other classrooms.

"Well, I guess that wasn't *too* painful," Pru admitted to ABE later in the evening as they left the gym. She'd checked first to make sure their parents were out of earshot behind them.

"Yeah. Mr. Jeffries seems nice. And funny."

"A little, I guess. He's an improvement over you-know-who at least." Pru stopped short, her eyes suddenly narrowed. "Oh, man. Speak of the devil."

ABE followed Pru's gaze. Mr. Jeffries was walking

down the hall toward them, but he wasn't alone. Mrs. Edleman walked by his side.

"Abe," Mrs. Edleman said, looking down over her glasses as they approached. "How nice to see you. And Prudence, of course."

"Hi, Mrs. Edleman," ABE said.

"Mrs. Edleman," Pru said. ABE imagined he could hear western showdown music in the background.

"Are these former students of yours, Mrs. Edleman?" Mr. Jeffries said. "How nice! I believe I have the pleasure of having them both in my homeroom. ABE and Prudence, isn't it? Sorry. I'm still learning names."

"It's *Pru*."

ABE didn't think Pru realized how snappish she sounded. Mrs. Edleman sort of had that effect on her.

"So, um, did you have a nice summer, Mrs. Edleman?" he said to change the subject.

"I did, Abraham, thank you for asking."

"It's . . . uh . . . I'm not . . ." That wasn't his name. ABE was an acronym, a nickname made from the initials of his real name, Aloysius Bartholomew Evans. Should he correct Mrs. Edleman? Before he could decide if it was okay to correct a teacher, his dad and Pru's mom stepped up behind them.

"Mrs. Edleman," Pru's mom said with a nod as she placed a hand on Pru's shoulder. Mrs. Edleman returned the nod.

"Mrs. Potts. Mr. Evans. A pleasure to see you both. Did you enjoy the open house?"

"We did," Pru's mom said. "In fact, we'd just finished up and were about to go get some ice cream. Gavin and ABE, would you like to join us?"

"Sounds good," ABE's dad said.

"Yeah," ABE agreed, admiring how quickly Pru's mom had managed to get them out of the chance encounter with Mrs. Edleman.

It just wasn't quick enough.

"Prudence," Mrs. Edleman said before they could make their escape, "just remember, this is a new year. That means a fresh start. I'm sure you will make the most of it. There's no need to repeat past mistakes and problem behaviors."

Pru's face turned bright red. ABE followed her gaze from Mrs. Edleman to Mr. Jeffries, and he saw their new teacher watching the exchange with raised eyebrows.

Pru was about to lose it. ABE needed to say something to distract her. What? He could ask Mr. Jeffries how he liked Middleton, since he was new to the school. Or was that a weird question to ask a teacher? He needed to say *something*.

"Let's go, Pru," her mother said, instead, rescuing Pru (and ABE).

ABE breathed a sigh of relief. Realizing that he was shifting his weight from foot to foot, he forced himself to stop. His mom always laughed when he did that, but in a nice way. She said it reminded her of when he was a toddler and just learning to walk. She said he would walk in place, like he couldn't decide which way to go.

"Mom, did you hear her?" Pru said when they'd walked a little way down the hall. "That was so embarrassing."

"I heard, honey. And I don't like it, either. But there's nothing to be done about it now. I'm sure it will blow over once the year starts."

Pru didn't say anything. She just looked back. ABE did, too. Mr. Jeffries and Mrs. Edleman were standing close together, talking. He saw Mrs. Edleman point in their direction—he was sure she had pointed at Pru. Mr. Jeffries frowned.

When ABE looked back at Pru, her face was still as red as her hair. He sighed.

Cell Block E might not be as easy to escape as they had hoped.

The air outside the ice-cream parlor smelled of a delicious combination of pine trees and the shop's special homemade hot fudge. ABE, his dad, and Pru's mom settled into a picnic table behind the store. Pru had gone back inside for napkins.

ABE looked up at the colored pennants that lined the picnic area. They flapped in the evening breeze. Gazing beyond the flags, ABE was disappointed to see clouds rolling in. He had hoped for a view of the stars.

"Why does the air always seem to smell so much better in the summer?" Pru's mother asked, inhaling deeply.

"Actually, it doesn't just seem to," ABE said. "It really does. I read an article about how odor molecules don't travel so well when it's cold, so there's not as much to smell."

"ABE, you are a marvel!" Pru's mother pointed her spoon at him. "You have so much knowledge floating around in that head of yours. Gavin, you must be so proud."

ABE looked at his dad, who blinked. "Yeah, he's a smart kid all right. Certainly doesn't get it from me. When I was his age all I cared about were sports and cars."

"He's been a good influence on Pru, that's for sure. I think she read more this summer than she has in the past . . . well, eleven years. Who'd have guessed she'd like mythology so much? Speaking of Pru . . ." Her mother paused to look around. "Where's she gotten to? How hard is it to find napkins?"

"I'm sure she'll be right out," ABE said.

"Yeah. It's an ice-cream parlor. How much trouble could she get into?" Pru's mother's eyes crinkled in a smile. “Then again, this *is* Pru we’re talking about. We might want to have the National Guard standing by.”

She and his dad laughed. Even ABE smiled.

“Maybe I should go check on her,” Pru’s mom said, setting her cup of ice cream on the table.

“I’ll go,” ABE said, glancing at his dad. “I, uh, want to use the bathroom anyway.”

As he walked around the building to the front entrance, he wondered if he should he have said *restroom* instead. Was the word *bathroom* impolite? What was proper etiquette when it came to lavatory terminology? *Lavatory!* Maybe he should have said that.

He was so lost in thought that he nearly walked right into Pru as she barreled around the corner.

“ABE,” she said, pulling him aside. “You’ll never guess what I just overheard! I was eavesdropping on a couple of teenagers—”

“You were eavesdropping on teenagers?”

Pru rolled her eyes. “Fine. I wasn’t *actually* eavesdropping. I was just interested in what they were talking about, so I stood someplace where I could be sure to accidentally overhear what they said. Okay?”

ABE wanted to point out that he hadn’t been objecting to eavesdropping. He’d just been surprised. But Pru seemed excited, so he stayed quiet.

“The point is, one of the teenagers has been working at Winterhaven House this summer. He was saying how crazy today had been up at the mansion because . . ."

Pru took a deep breath. She gripped his shoulders.

"Because they're getting ready for Old Man Grimnir's return tomorrow. ABE, *Odin is coming back*!"

ABE WOKE UP THE NEXT DAY TO A SKY THE COLOR OF MOURNING. THE BOOK he'd been reading when he fell asleep—a collection of Norse myths—lay closed on his bedside table. He guessed that his mom had placed it there after she came home. She always checked in on him when she worked a late shift.

He dressed and paused outside his parents' room on his way downstairs, wondering if they were up and if he had time to say hi to his mom before going to meet Pru. He was about to knock when he heard his father's voice on the other side of the door.

"It was fine, I guess. A little dull. What can you expect? It's school. But I'll tell you, Maddie, I'm worried about the boy. Last night, one kid laughed at him and his old teacher called him the wrong name. ABE didn't say or do anything. It's like the kid doesn't even know how to stand up for himself. It was painful to watch."

ABE pulled his hand back from the door. It hung in the air a moment before he lowered it to his side and went downstairs. He'd leave them a note. They were used to him and Pru spending the day together.

As ABE passed the front door, he heard an urgent rapping that announced Pru's early arrival.

"Are you ready?" she asked when he opened the door.

"Just about." He sat on the bottom step of the staircase and wiggled one foot into a sneaker, pulling on the heel flap when it got squished into the shoe. He had new sneakers in a box in his bedroom. But those were for the first day of school. He didn't feel right about wearing them before then.

Pru paced back and forth outside the screen door. She rubbed her hands together with glee.

"Can you believe it, ABE? Odin is here in Middleton again! I wonder what brought him back."

"You don't think he wants the Eye of Odin back, do you? It was his actual eye, after all. Maybe he's mad we hid it."

Pru paused. She chewed her lower lip. It was a new habit. Her hair had grown in the past year. It no longer fell in a bob around her chin, so it wasn't as easily accessible for chewing.

"No," she said, resuming her pacing. "He went centuries without his eye. I bet he doesn't even miss it anymore. And besides, *we* didn't hide the Eye. Mister Fox did. If Odin wants to be mad at Mister Fox, then that's fine with me. He can get in line."

After a quick dash to grab a granola bar from the kitchen, ABE opened the door to join Pru on the porch. Glancing at the leaden sky, he went back in to grab an umbrella.

"Anything *else* you want to do before we go?" Pru asked.

"Ah, no. I'm good," he said, following Pru as she set off. He tried to match her brisk pace. "Um, Pru, what do you think is going to happen when we get there? I mean, it's exciting that Odin is back. But we don't even know if he'll want to see us."

Pru didn't say anything at first. Instead, she chewed her lip again.

"I know," she said. "But at least his being back is *something.* You know? He *has* to see us."

Pru quickened their pace even more as the sky began a slow leak. ABE opened his umbrella. Around them, tear-shaped drops of rain fell from the clouds above, completing ABE's sense of foreboding about what they might find when they finally reached Winterhaven House.

✳

They needn't have worried about getting in to see Odin. Two sights greeted them at the mansion's iron gates. The first was a sign announcing that the building and grounds were temporarily closed while the museum underwent renovations.

That might have presented a problem if not for the second sight. A broad-shouldered woman with a long blonde braid stood on the other side of the gate. She appeared to be waiting for them, unbothered by the rain.

"Hilde!" Pru called as she broke into a run.

Odin's assistant reached down and unlocked the gate. She swung it open to admit Pru and ABE.

"Hello, children."

"Hi, Hilde," ABE said, catching up and holding his umbrella up higher to try to cover everyone. "Why are you standing out in the rain?"

"I'm waiting for you, of course." A hint of a smile showed on Hilde's usually stern face.

"Waiting for us?" Pru repeated. "Why? How? Wait! Don't tell me. Is 'Mr. Grimnir' *expecting* us again?"

Hilde's smile slipped from her face as though washed off by the falling rain.

"This is not a time for jokes, children. Come with

me. Odin *is* expecting you. But he does not wait with good news."

"What's wrong?" ABE asked.

"That is for Odin to say."

They walked in silence across the gravel drive and through Winterhaven's halls, where ABE's eyes followed the frozen march of the Viking warriors carved into the towering stone walls of the mansion. He watched them disappear down corridors not taken.

Hilde led them to the same room where they'd had their first audience with Odin. It was empty this time, though. Hilde said she would return with "the others" shortly and left them with instructions to wait as she exited through a different door.

Pru threw her arms out wide as soon as Hilde had closed the door behind her. "We're back!" she exclaimed, clearly not fazed by Hilde's somber mood.

"Six chairs," ABE said, walking around the long table that ran the length of the room.

"What?" Pru asked.

"There are six chairs." ABE gestured to the setup. He recognized one of the chairs, a high-backed and intricately carved wooden seat at the head of the table. It was the chair Odin had sat in on their last visit.

"There's the two of us plus Odin and Hilde," Pru said, considering. "That's four."

"Hilde said she'd be back with 'the others.' I wonder who the last two chairs are for."

"Maybe Thor's back, too."

"Maybe. I kind of hope not, though."

"What? Are you crazy? Thor's awesome!"

"No, I know. It's not that I don't want to see him. I do. Thor saved our lives. He's great!"

"Then what's wrong?"

ABE turned to one of the narrow windows that lined the wall. "It's the rain. Last night, I noticed that clouds had rolled in. I didn't think anything of it at first. Then you found out Odin was back."

"And you wondered if maybe Thor was back, too." Pru frowned. She'd been practically dancing through the room. Now she slowed down. ABE guessed she was arriving at the same conclusion he'd reached.

"We know that the weather can reflect Thor's mood, right?" he said. "We got all those clouds last year because Thor was mad about being locked up. But, even with everything that happened then, it never rained. The clouds today remind me of the clouds last time. With the rain, though, and Hilde's mood . . . everything seems . . . I don't know. Sad."

Pru opened her mouth as if to argue. But she closed it again without saying anything and joined ABE at the window. A chill filled the room, despite the fire that burned in the hearth and the flaming torches that lined the walls.

ABE had wondered about the torches last time. Now, knowing what he did about Mythics and their incompatibility with technology, he supposed that torches made sense for a room where gods gathered and held council.

"What do you think has happened?" Pru asked. She drew her finger across the glass of the window. Beads of moisture gathered on her fingertip.

"I don't know . . . but I think we might be about to find out," he said as Thor's booming voice reached them from behind the door through which Hilde had left.

"And so they must carry the weight of our inaction?" Thor demanded of someone.

The door burst open and the god of thunder stormed into the room. His presence charged the air with a current of anger and tension that raised the hairs on ABE's arms.

"Thor!" Pru exclaimed, taking a step toward him. She stopped in her tracks as Thor turned his fierce glare in their direction.

Seeing them, the god's brow smoothed a bit.

"Children, forgive me. Hilde mentioned you had arrived. It is good to see you again." Thor's mustache and beard parted in what looked like an attempt at a smile. He took a deep breath. The atmosphere in the room lightened a little, but Thor's clenched fists and the corded muscles of his arms betrayed his tense emotion.

"What's wrong?" Pru asked.

"A great many things." Thor glanced back at the door. The wood along the upper hinge had splintered, and the door hung limply in its frame. Thor closed his eyes and took another deep breath. "All of which we shall discuss, and soon. First, though, I have yet to greet the brave lad who recovered the Eye of Odin from the field of battle during our last meeting."

Thor approached ABE and gripped his shoulder. ABE's eyes widened and he clenched his jaw shut to keep from crying out. Thor's grip was iron! Why did he even bother carrying a hammer around? His pinkie could probably drive a railroad stake through the ground!

"Yup. He's the brave lad, all right," Pru said, her eyes dancing. Thor's arrival had restored at least some of her good humor. "Did you know his name—*Aloysius*—means 'famous warrior'?"

"A fine name for such a . . . strapping young lad!"

ABE looked down at his scrawny frame. "That's, ah, very nice, sir. But ABE's fine. Really."

"But your true name has such strong meaning, lad!

And it fits someone with the courage to charge into a field of frost giants. You should embrace your fierce nature!"

Pru started nodding vigorously.

"*Yes.* Yes, ABE, that is exactly what you should be doing. I am *always* telling him to embrace his fierce nature," she confided to Thor.

ABE cast a sidelong glance at Pru. She responded with a look of innocence. At least ABE assumed she was trying to look innocent. Not having had a lot of practice actually *being* innocent, she wasn't pulling it off too well.

"Blustering oaf," a voice muttered, interrupting the exchange.

A bent old man entered the room, carefully navigating through the damaged door. ABE turned to Pru in amazement when he recognized the newcomer. Her dropped jaw reflected the surprise he knew must show on his own face.

Odin, Allfather of the gods of the North, god of wisdom and war, shuffled into the room. He leaned heavily on a long wooden walking stick. A blue cloak lay across his stooped shoulders. Every few steps, Odin reached out with one hand to gather the cloak at his neck as if it were a shawl. The wide, broad-brimmed hat atop his head bobbed up and down as unsteady steps carried him across the room.

"Go, children," Thor whispered. "Stand behind your seats. Sit after he does. Speak when addressed and do not test my father's patience. I have already lost my temper with him once this morning and I should not have done so. These are troubled times."

ABE followed Thor's directions. Odin hadn't seemed this weak and old the last time he and Pru saw him. What had happened?

The Allfather made his way to the seat at the head of the table, and Thor moved to stand behind the chair to his father's right. Hilde returned to the room and stood across from ABE and next to Thor. ABE glanced at the empty seat at the foot of the table.

Odin's chair slid across the floor and the god dropped into it, muttering. He removed his hat and hung it off the back of his throne-like seat.

ABE, Pru, and the others also sat.

"We are here because of betrayal," Odin wheezed, looking at everyone around the table. "We are here because of trickery! We are here . . . because of death."

ABE's stomach sank with dread.

"My son is dead!" Odin's declaration came in a hoarse gasp. "Baldur, the best of us, is dead."

ABE clutched the table to steady himself. The room swayed in the flickering torchlight. Everything seemed suddenly less stable and less sure.

"Oh no!" Pru said. "I'm so sorry."

ABE heard empathy in her voice, the empathy of someone who had also lost a loved one. But she didn't really understand. She hadn't read and reread the Norse myths like he had. If she had, she wouldn't be sad.

She'd be terrified.

"That's it, then?" ABE said, forgetting Thor's instructions not to speak. "It's started?"

"What's started?" Pru asked.

"Ragnarok," ABE said, looking at her. "Ragnarok has started, Pru. It's the end of the world."

CHAPTER 5

"WHAT ARE YOU TALKING ABOUT?" PRU DEMANDED OF ABE. SHE TURNED TO Odin. "What's he talking about? What does he mean, Ragnarok has started?"

"Let your friend tell you," Odin said. "Like you, he seems unable to hold his tongue, even when instructed to do so."

ABE flinched at the reprimand, but he didn't let that stop him from answering. He spoke quickly as his words tried to keep pace with the fear building inside him.

"You know how the Norse myths work," he began. "Some of them are stories about things that have happened. But because Odin drank from the Well of Wisdom and gained the ability to see the future, some

Norse myths are stories about things that haven't happened yet but will. They're stories that came from what Odin saw in his visions. One of those myths is of Ragnarok, the end of all things."

"I *know* all that. But what makes you think Ragnarok has started?"

"Because Ragnarok doesn't just end in death. It *starts* with death, too. Baldur's death. Loki kills Baldur, the favorite of the gods. Then Loki runs away from Asgard. Thor finds him and brings him back to be judged and imprisoned. Loki eventually breaks free and all the giants join him to fight the gods. And everyone on Asgard and on our world dies in that war. *Everyone!* That's how the stories go."

Pru nodded, her lower lip tucked under her front teeth. "I remember now. But can't we do something? I mean, I knew Ragnarok was coming . . . someday—but not now! Can't we change what's going to happen?"

"The fates hold us tight, child," Thor said. "But—"

"Change what is going to happen?" Odin interrupted. He leaned forward. "We cannot *change* the future. We should not want to! Your clever friend is wrong. Not *everyone* dies. Tell the story true, boy."

ABE frowned. "He's right, I guess. There are supposed to be a *few* survivors among people and gods. But hardly any—"

"Yes," Odin said, interrupting again. "And in time

those survivors will rebuild Asgard and Midgard. But they will make better worlds, untouched by evil. Because through the sacrifice of the gods, all giants and monsters will be destroyed during Ragnarok. Imagine that, boy! A world without evil! It will be a most terrible triumph."

"Triumph? But so many will die," Pru said.

"All things die, even gods. What matters is *how* we die. And, more, how we are remembered. The gods of Asgard will not be remembered as cowards who hid from their fate."

"So there's nothing we can do?" ABE asked. "No hope?"

"There has never been hope. Only fate and duty and death."

A long stretch of silence followed Odin's words, during which the dim stone room felt like a tomb.

A soft rumble in the sky above broke the silence. Thor shifted in his seat.

"My father is right, of course. Our fate is set. And yet . . . while there may not be hope, there may yet be time."

Odin snorted. Thor did not look in his direction but continued.

"The lad was right in his accounting of events. Loki has killed Baldur and now he has fled. He must be found and imprisoned. Honor and justice demand it. But that imprisonment will take place in Asgard. Remember that time passes differently there. Loki's imprisonment may last hundreds or thousands of your years."

Thor's words offered a little comfort. But ABE still felt the weight of Ragnarok—of all that death—pressing down on him.

"Listen to Thor, the hero of Asgard," Odin mocked in his withered and withering voice. "He whose mighty hands wield Mjolnir would hide behind the hands of a clock. What does it matter if Ragnarok comes in a day or a thousand days? My son is dead! I will have his killer brought to justice. And you—*all of you*—will help me!"

"Us?" Pru asked.

"Yes. I have seen the moment of Loki's capture. All of you in this room will be present for it. All of you . . . and one other," Odin said a moment before someone knocked.

The sound came from the door through which ABE and Pru had entered (the one still on its hinges).

"Who?" ABE asked, but he was interrupted by the sound of Pru's gasp.

"*I knew it!*" she said.

"Knew what?" ABE looked from Pru to the door as the handle began to turn.

"ABE, think about it! Middleton is filled with Mythics again. That can only mean one thing!"

The door opened and light spilled in, revealing the silhouette of a single figure. As ABE's eyes adjusted to the brightness, he made out the shape of a tall man. The twin peaks of his hat stood up almost like ears, and the tail of his long coat hung below his knees.

"Mister Fox!"

The detective strode into the room. He looked exactly as he had the last time they'd seen him. *Exactly.* ABE wondered if Mister Fox had just the one hat and coat or a bunch of identical ones.

"Sorry to interrupt. I assume my invitation to this little get-together got lost in the mail. Don't worry, it happens. Here's a tip. Use *domovye* for all your future postal needs, especially where invitations are concerned," Mister Fox said, referring to the Russian household spirits that also lived in the Henhouse. "That's what I do."

Pru grabbed ABE's sleeve. He didn't need to look at her to know she was smiling. He was, too!

Any misgivings he might have once had about seeing Mister Fox again vanished. Considering what they faced—the literal end of the world—there was no one he would have rather had walk through that door and start rambling. And, boy, was he rambling!

"Of course, you can run into a small problem with *domovye*," Mister Fox continued. "Every once in a while, your message will end up in someone's shoe.

But that's the *domovye* for you. *Weird* fascination with shoes." Reaching the table and resting his elbows on the back of the empty chair, Mister Fox leaned forward and said, "Hello, Pru. Hi, ABE."

"Hi, Mister Fox," ABE said.

Pru grunted.

ABE looked at her, eyebrows raised.

Oh right.

This was Pru. She wasn't going to let Mister Fox off the hook *that* easily for staying away so long.

"Who is this?" Hilde asked.

"Excellent!" Mister Fox exclaimed, snapping his fingers. "Names. It's usually a good idea to begin with names. That's what I always say. You can avoid so much trouble if you just figure out names right from the start. Isn't that true, Pru?"

"*I'm* not talking to you, Mister Stay-Away-for-a-Whole-Year."

Mister Fox sucked his breath in between his teeth. "Ooh, close. Very close. But, no. It's Mister *Fox* not Mister Stay-Away-for-a-Whole-Year. You were half right, though. Well done, Pru. Excellent memory, almost."

Pru squeaked in protest.

ABE wanted to laugh. Mister Fox was in top form. How was he always so confident? It didn't matter. *He was back*. Just when they needed him most, Mister Fox was back! If anyone could find Loki and help imprison him in Asgard, Mister Fox could.

"I'd be glad to finish introductions," Mister Fox said as ABE relaxed into his seat, "but I'm afraid I'm on a tight schedule and can't stay."

"What?" ABE sat up straight again.

"I'm leaving. And you two are coming with me."

"We can't leave," Pru said. "You don't understand! Baldur is dead. Ragnarok is coming."

"I know," Mister Fox said. He removed his hat and spoke to Odin. "For what it's worth, I'm sorry for your loss. I truly am. I met Baldur once in my youth. He was kind to me."

"Then you should want his murderer captured!" Thor said, slapping the table.

"And you're so sure that's Loki?" Mister Fox said, turning his gaze on Thor.

Thor froze, stunned. "What?"

"You sound sure that Loki killed Baldur. Why? Did you see him do it?"

Thor's face turned red and he scratched his beard. "I was, ah, distracted."

"Very distracted from what I heard. According to my source, the circumstances around Baldur's death were fairly chaotic. It happened in the middle of a wild celebration."

Thor said nothing. Instead, he cast a guilty look at

Odin. The Allfather, however, kept his one eye on Mister Fox.

"What 'source'?" Hilde asked. "How do you know this?"

"Good question," Mister Fox said. "I like that. Let's just say a little bird told me. Well . . . a furry little bird. Kind of ratty looking. No wings, but a long, bushy tail and a worrisome penchant for inappropriate language. That kind of little bird."

"Ratatosk!" ABE said.

"We've kept in touch," Mister Fox agreed with a shrug.

"My father saw my brother's death!" Thor said, recovering from his embarrassment. "He saw long ago that Loki would kill Baldur."

Mister Fox stood up straight and slipped his hands into his pockets. "Yes. Your father had a vision of the future. In that vision, Loki kills Baldur. Now, because of that vision, we're supposed to condemn Loki. But here's the problem. Nobody saw Loki commit the act in the present. And the last time we crossed paths with him, Loki was trying to get the Eye of Odin so he could see a way to *change* his future. So I have to ask . . . what if Odin's vision was wrong?"

Thor also stood. A low, threatening peal of thunder rolled outside. "My father's visions have never been wrong."

"There's a first time for everything."

ABE looked from Thor to Mister Fox. What was happening? Why were they arguing? They were supposed to be on the same side!

"You think Loki is *innocent*?" Hilde said, eyes wide with disbelief.

"I don't know," Mister Fox said with another shrug. "Not for sure. But that's the point. None of us know anything for sure. You're all making assumptions based on a vision. That's not justice. That's a witch hunt. I have a particular objection to witch hunts, by the way."

"This is madness!" Thor roared, banging his fist on the table. "You would stand there and defend Loki when we have all witnessed his mischief and evildoing? He was my friend once. But even I see that time has passed. He must be caught and brought to justice. He *will* be! My father has seen it!"

"Well, good luck with that. We're leaving. Let's go, Pru and ABE."

"You will *not* leave this council!" Thor commanded. Thunder rumbled outside, like a drumroll's call to battle.

"Sit down, boy," Odin said, waving Thor back into his seat.

Thor pressed his eyes closed. The cords in his neck tightened as if his head wanted to blast off from his body and soar into orbit. After a moment, though, he collapsed into his seat, arms folded.

All eyes turned to the Allfather, who had kept otherwise silent through the exchange. Though Odin continued to address his words to Thor, his eye remained fixed on Mister Fox.

"The witch's foundling's words do not matter. He is a child who is frightened of his fate and hides in his religion of uncertainty and disbelief. Let him go. Let them all go."

Odin flicked his hands in a gesture of dismissal.

"But, Father . . ." Thor said.

"Hush, boy. It does not matter. Nothing they do matters."

ABE rose as Mister Fox jerked his thumb in the direction of the door. Pru followed a moment later after muttering "Sorry" to Thor. It wasn't until she and ABE had covered half the distance to the exit that Mister Fox also turned to leave. Odin called out to them one last time before they reached the door.

"This changes nothing. You—all of you—will be there at the moment of Loki's discovery and you will assist in his capture. I have seen it," Odin said, straining his voice until it broke into either a cough or a laugh, ABE wasn't sure which. "You cannot change the future!"

"Don't be so sure," Mister Fox said, closing the door on the gods.

*

Pru burst through the front doors of Winterhaven House, leaving ABE and Mister Fox in her wake.

"Is it me or does Pru seem upset about something?" the detective asked ABE in a near whisper.

"Yes, she's upset about something. And, yes, it's you." That was all the warning ABE could give Mister Fox before Pru spun around.

"*Where have you been?*" she demanded.

"I thought you weren't talking to me?"

"I'm not. I'm yelling at you. It's completely different."

"Ah."

"No, seriously! Where were you? You said we'd see you again."

"And now you have!" Mister Fox said with a bow and a flourish of his hat. "You see? I always keep my word—eventually."

Pru muttered something impolite that made it clear she'd spent far too much time in Ratatosk's company.

Mister Fox relented. "I know I've been gone a long time. I'm sorry for that. But it couldn't be avoided. It's a big world, and there were other problems that had to be dealt with, other mysteries that had to be solved. My job keeps me hopping."

ABE laughed.

Pru and Mister Fox turned to him.

"Uh . . . sorry. I thought that was a joke. 'Hopping'?

You know, because the Henhouse hops around on a giant chicken foot."

Pru groaned while Mister Fox grinned at ABE.

"Sorry," ABE said again. "Yelling makes me a little nervous."

"Anyway," Pru continued, "you've been gone a year. Then you come back just when things are getting interesting, and you say we can't be part of the adventure. It's not fair!"

"I said nothing of the sort. Just because Odin and I don't see eye to eye—"

ABE gave another nervous laugh, and Pru looked at him with an exasperated expression.

"Eye to eye?" ABE repeated. "Because of the Eye of Odin? Never mind."

Pru shook her head. "Seriously, ABE. *Timing.*"

"Sorry," he said. Clearly, Pru didn't appreciate a good pun.

"As I was saying," Mr. Fox went on, "just because Odin and I don't . . . agree . . . on what needs to happen next doesn't mean there isn't work for us to do. Let Thor and Hilde try to find and punish Loki. We three have another task."

"What?" Pru asked.

"Visit me tomorrow at the Henhouse. We'll discuss it then."

LYING IN BED THAT NIGHT, ABE COULDN'T TURN HIS MIND OFF. HE WENT BACK and forth between worrying about Ragnarok and wondering what Mister Fox had planned for them. His thoughts kept him awake late into the night. He'd only just drifted off when a knock woke him.

"Mom?" he mumbled, rolling over.

He sat up when he heard the knock again. He rubbed his eyes. Weird. The sound hadn't come from his bedroom door. Had he dreamt it?

Knock, knock.

Pulling his covers up to his chin, ABE swallowed. The sound was *inside* his room. It had come from the foot of his bed.

It was at that unfortunate moment in the darkness

of his bedroom on a cloudy, starless night that a thought occurred to ABE: if Mythics were real, then were monsters under the bed real, too?

And did they knock?

ABE crept to the bottom of his bed and peered over the footboard.

Sitting among a pile of recently finished books was the box shaped like a miniature Henhouse he had received from Mister Fox. It shone with a pale blue glow. The light seeped through the cracks between the house's siding and through the small window above the door.

The knocking came again. It came, without question, from the miniature Henhouse.

"Okay. This is new. You never glowed before. Or knocked. So I should probably open you, right? When a box starts making knocking noises that's probably what it wants, I guess. Okay. So I'll open you. Because this isn't creepy or weird at all."

ABE lifted the Henhouse onto his bed and reached toward the clasp that held the box shut. It had been designed so that the Henhouse could swing open on hinges along a break that split the front half of the house from the back half, like a dollhouse. His hands paused a moment on the metal. It felt warm. Taking a deep breath, ABE undid the clasp and opened the box.

"ABE! It's about time! How soundly do you sleep?"

ABE scrambled back in shock, his blankets bunching beneath him.

The looking glass he'd received from Mister Fox hung suspended inside, as expected. Unexpectedly, however, the detective's face looked up at him from the enchanted mirror. A nimbus of orange light surrounded him.

"Mister Fox?"

"Were you expecting someone else?"

"What? No! I wasn't expecting anyone at all. You can talk to me through this?"

"Yes. It's a variation on scrying, like I showed you at the Henhouse last year. It's one of the enchantments worked into the looking glass. Listen, there's not much time—"

"Does Pru know?"

At the mention of her name, the image of Mister Fox in the looking glass wavered. An image of Pru replaced it.

"ABE! How cool is this? We can talk to each other through these and . . . wait." Pru covered her mouth with her hands. ABE could tell she was trying (unsuccessfully) to hide a smile. "ABE, are those tie-dyed pajamas?"

"Oh! Ah . . . yeah. Sorry. Um . . . are those unicorns on yours?"

Pru yelped and dove out of sight just as Mister Fox's image reasserted itself.

"We don't have time for this. If I didn't have my hands full right now, we'd be having a very serious conversation about the misuse of magical artifacts. Well, first we'd talk about Pru's surprising fascination with unicorns. But *then* we'd have a serious conversation about artifacts."

"Is something wrong?" ABE asked.

"You could say that. Trolls are attacking Winterhaven House."

Only then did ABE understand the whole meaning of the image in the looking glass. The orange glow behind Mister Fox was not part of the enchantment that allowed them to communicate. It was fire.

"Are you okay?"

"Of course. It's not my time. It's you two I'm worried about. I want you both someplace safe. Go to the Henhouse. I'm on my way, but I don't want you to wait. Pru, you know the way in."

"But what about our parents?" ABE asked.

"Your parents should be fine. In fact, I think they'll be safer without you two there. Trolls are attracted to treasure, especially magical treasure. Your looking glasses are two of the most powerful objects in this town right now. Your families should be safe once you leave. But I've convinced some of the *domovye* to keep an eye on your houses, just to be sure. The rest will escort you to the cemetery. Now go, and take your looking glasses with you!"

The connection broke, and Mister Fox's image faded from the glass.

ABE leapt off his bed and dressed. He grabbed his phone just as it rang.

"You're there!" Pru's relief was clear. "Are you okay?"

"Yeah. I was about to leave. I'll see you at the Henhouse?"

"Let's meet at the Earth Center. It's on the way for both of us. We can go to the Henhouse together from there."

"Good idea," ABE said before hanging up. He hadn't liked the idea of walking to the cemetery alone.

Looking glass in hand, ABE grabbed his windbreaker from his closet and slipped downstairs. Goose bumps rose on the back of his neck as he stepped out into the night air. He zipped up his jacket. At the end of his walkway, he hesitated, still anxious about his parents' safety.

Mister Fox had said he'd send *domovye*. But they were mostly invisible. ABE wondered how he would know when they got there. Should he wait?

He caught himself shifting his weight from foot to foot and forced himself to stop. Instead, he tightened his grip on his looking glass. The familiar polished wood of the handle comforted him. He had never admitted it to Pru, but he felt like a wizard whenever he held it.

The looking glass, of course!

Kicking himself for not thinking of it right away, ABE lifted the glass to his eye and peered through the magnifying side. After all, the *domovye* were household spirits. That made them Mythics. They should be visible through the enchanted glass.

Light flared as ABE looked through the device and dozens of figures appeared, lit by the golden glow that surrounded Mythics when viewed through the glass.

ABE had read about *domovye* after meeting Mister Fox, so he was somewhat prepared for their bizarre appearance. Despite being called spirits, there was nothing ghostlike about the creatures around him. They looked like small men (just a little taller than ABE) with thick walrus moustaches that blended into even thicker gray beards.

ABE had learned that *domovye* often adopted the look of the master or mistress of their house. Sure enough, the *domovye* all wore the same coat and hat that Mister Fox wore—only their clothing was almost cartoonishly big. The oversized brims of their hats and their buttoned coats and upturned collars hid most of their bodies.

The *domovye* avoided open spaces. They crouched in patches of darkness between buildings and seemed to have a fondness for climbing. ABE saw one *domovoi* scale the side of a house to perch beside a chimney. It moved with the skill of a jungle ape. Another one had crouched beneath a tree close to ABE. He approached it.

"So . . . you guys will stay and watch over my mom and dad?" he asked.

The figure nodded.

"Okay. Thanks."

ABE took one last look at his house before hurrying off to meet Pru, a dozen *domovye* following closely behind. He tried very hard not to think about the trolls out there, somewhere in the night.

CHAPTER 7

ABE WAS GLAD FOR THE COMPANY OF THE *DOMOVYE* AS HE MADE HIS WAY through the deserted streets of Middleton. The night seemed particularly quiet. Granted, he was not used to walking the town's streets in the hours after midnight. But he had expected to see *some* signs of life. An occasional car. A light in a window.

Instead, Middleton appeared deserted.

A ghost town.

ABE smiled despite his discomfort as the phrase sprang to mind. After all, his companions were actual spirits—in name, anyway. He lifted his looking glass to his eye to reassure himself that the *domovye* were still there.

Strange. Were there fewer of them than the last time he'd checked?

He hurried on.

He found Pru waiting for him at the Earth Center. It was weird being there with her again. They had both avoided the place for months after their adventure with the Eye of Odin. It had reminded them too much of Loki. But ABE believed in the center's environmental mission, so he had gone back to volunteering after a while. Pru had stayed away.

"It's about time," Pru said as ABE approached.

"Sorry. I wanted to make sure the *domovye* showed up before I left my parents alone."

"Are they cool, or what?" A quick smile lit Pru's face. "I'd only seen their hands before. The way they look and move—it's like someone crossed Mister Fox and a monkey!"

"That's a mental image that will stick with me."

"Glad I could help." Pru's shoulders relaxed a little. "I'm glad you're here. It was creepy waiting by myself. Come on. Let's go."

They set off for Main Street, which ran all the way from Winterhaven House through town and down to the cemetery. They'd only traveled a couple of blocks when Pru paused. She held her looking glass to her eye.

"ABE, I thought you said you waited for the *domovye* before you left your house."

"I did."

"Didn't any come with you?"

"Yeah. About a dozen. Why?"

"That's not possible. I had about that many with me, too. But now I can only see a handful."

"What?" ABE lifted his own glass. He counted six, maybe seven, *domovye* in the area. What had happened to the rest?

"ABE," Pru hissed. "Look!"

ABE turned in the direction she pointed. The looking glass framed a shadow in the distance. His stomach lurched as the enchanted lens zoomed in on the shadow. It magnified and sharpened the image in the glass.

A troll!

ABE shuddered. Trolls were *awful* looking. They were worse than giants. Giants at least looked like people (even if they were really big). Trolls were something else. The brute before them had two heads—*two heads!*—and at least four arms. Though not as tall as a giant, the troll still stood a couple of feet taller than the biggest person ABE had ever met. Hair (or was it fur?) covered its massively wide chest and a loincloth hung from its waist.

As ABE watched, two *domovye* launched themselves at the troll. The creature howled and reached for a nearby stop sign. It tore the sign—and a good bit of sidewalk—from the ground with a shrug of its massive shoulders. Swinging the makeshift club, it struck one of its attackers and sent it tumbling hat over coattail across the ground. As it rolled, the *domovoi* grew increasingly less solid until it vanished from sight completely.

"Did that *domovoi* just die?" Pru said. "*Can* domovye *die*?"

"I don't know. But we sure can! Come on, let's get to the Henhouse!"

Pru nodded. ABE took one last glance at the troll through the looking glass. The remaining *domovye* had taken their fallen companion's place and were swarming the beast.

"ABE, come on!"

He forced himself to look away and followed Pru. They turned onto Main Street, and ABE wondered how much time the remaining *domovye* could buy them.

A popping sound behind him soon offered the first hint.

"The streetlights are going out!" Pru said. "Why?"

"The troll must have defeated the *domovye*," ABE said, struggling to keep up with Pru. "Mister Fox said Mythics and technology don't mix. I think the troll is chasing us and the lights are going out as he passes them!"

He looked back—and immediately wished he

hadn't. The troll was using its multiple arms as additional legs and was closing in on them fast!

Beside ABE, Pru stopped short.

"What's wrong?" he asked, turning back to tug on her arm. "We have to go!"

"No," Pru said, standing up straight. "We can't keep running."

"Yes, we can! It's easy. I'll show you!"

"We won't make it, ABE. The troll is too fast. Besides, we're Fibbers! These looking glasses can send the troll back to wherever it comes from, right? So let's send it on its way."

ABE stared at her. She was serious. And insane.

And kind of amazing.

"I think this is a terrible idea," he said, moving to stand beside her.

"You think *all* my ideas are terrible," she said. He knew she was trying to sound brave, but her voice shook.

The troll had slowed when its prey stopped moving, perhaps sensing a trap. Or maybe it was just stunned by what it considered to be a truly astounding display of stupidity. It stood in the middle of Main Street, about a dozen yards away. The Laundromat was to its left, and the barbershop ABE went to get his hair cut was on its right. He would *never* look at those places the same way again.

Assuming he and Pru survived.

The troll snorted. It resumed its bizarre loping movement—slowly at first, but it soon picked up speed.

Pru raised her arm and pointed the looking glass toward the troll.

The troll continued to move closer. ABE felt the muscles of his neck tighten. Why hadn't it vanished? How close did it need to be?

"Pru . . . it's not working!"

"It *has* to work!" She wiggled her looking glass the way one might shake a TV remote with failing batteries.

The troll leapt at them with all four arms outstretched.

"ABE, run!" Pru shouted.

Pru dodged to the right as ABE dodged left.

One of the troll's heads turned to follow ABE's movement, and the other followed Pru. Its attention split, the troll landed clumsily on the ground and tumbled over itself, its limbs instantly entangled. Pru ducked into a narrow alley as ABE scrambled to hide behind the florist's delivery van, parked on the side of the road.

He peeked around the back of the van just in time to see the troll stand back up and, after a moment of indecision, chase after Pru.

He had to do something! But what? Their looking glasses hadn't worked.

Well, Pru's hadn't. He hadn't tried his. But why would his work if Pru's didn't?

The troll reached the opening of the alley, but its massive frame proved too wide for the narrow space. Luckily, the creature seemed too dumb to try to turn sideways. Apparently, two heads *weren't* better than one.

ABE groaned. Pru was right. He really needed to work on the appropriateness of his timing with puns.

Wait! Two heads!

The troll had two heads. The looking glasses worked by magnifying a Mythic's sense that it didn't belong on Earth. But maybe to work, *both* of the troll's heads would have to look into the enchanted mirrors. Two heads probably meant two brains.

He peeked at the troll again. It tore at the brickwork at the mouth of the alley with terrifying efficiency. Chunks of masonry and dust flew from its four jackhammer-like hands as it beat at the opening of Pru's safe haven.

The troll still hadn't tried turning sideways.

Two *very small* brains, ABE decided. But his idea still made sense.

He rounded the van and tiptoed into the street. Somehow, he had to get Pru's attention without letting the troll see him. He had to be as quiet as a—

Clank!

ABE froze as the metallic clang filled the air. He looked at his feet. A steel road plate lay on the ground beneath him. The road crew that had put it there (probably to cover an area of construction) must have placed it poorly, because it had shifted under the weight of ABE's step and banged against the concrete.

Swallowing past the lump in his throat, ABE looked up just in time to see one of the troll's heads turn toward him. A large blob of drool pooled on the beast's lower lip as it curled in a snarl. The drop fell, and before it could even hit the ground, the troll lunged in ABE's direction. ABE retreated until his back pressed against the florist's van.

"Hey, ugly!" Pru called, stepping out from the alley. "Leave him alone!"

One of the troll's heads stayed oriented on ABE while the other head turned toward Pru. Torn by conflicting desires, the troll stalled in the middle of the street.

"Pru!" ABE called. "Two heads! I think we both have to use our looking glasses!"

"Right!" she agreed as the troll howled in frustration. The muscles in its legs coiled, signaling that it was ready to pounce.

ABE lifted his looking glass at the same moment Pru did. There was a flash of light. When it faded, the troll had vanished into a cloud of shimmering gold sparks.

ABE and Pru lowered their glasses. Walking slowly, they met in the middle of the street. They stopped in the exact spot where the troll had stood, moments before.

ABE couldn't believe it. The plan had worked.

"We're safe," he said. Relief spread over him in a wave of soothing warmth.

That's when a truck screeched around the corner and, catching their startled faces in its high beams, barreled directly at them.

CHAPTER 8

A ROOSTER CROWED.

ABE's eyes fluttered open.

He floated in a cloud of softness, embraced by cool linens. His head rested on a pillow so fluffed with down that someone could have put a whole bag of frozen peas beneath it and no princess would ever have known.

He spread his arms and legs wide, sinking deeper into the marshmallow mattress that held him, basking in the comforts of his home and bed.

Except his bed wasn't that soft.

Or that big.

He sat up in a flash as the events of the night before came back to him. He remembered his flight from home and the troll and then, just when he had thought they were safe, the headlights that had borne down on him and Pru and . . .

His head sank back into the pillow. He sighed in relief as the rest of the evening came back in a rush.

The truck that had nearly hit them had been driven by Mister Fox. He'd swerved at the last moment, and the truck had spun into a streetlight. Mister Fox had escaped unharmed. Rather than send them home, he'd brought them back to the Henhouse.

The Henhouse.

ABE sat up once more. A smile spread across his face. He pulled himself out of bed, surprised by how smooth the wooden floor felt beneath his bare feet. Light streamed in through a large stained-glass window that displayed an image of Stonehenge.

He pressed his hand to the glass, wondering if it would feel warm. Was it real sunlight? He couldn't be sure. The Henhouse was an impossibility. Mister Fox described it as a series of houses all occupying the same space.

That would have made some sense if each house were a little smaller than the one that contained it. But the witch Baba Yaga had built the Henhouse. She had used her magic to put the larger versions of the Henhouse *inside* the smaller ones. That meant the Henhouse grew in size the deeper one went.

Considering the size of his room, ABE had to be

pretty far inside the Henhouse. So how could the light be actual sunlight? But the window was, indeed, warm. ABE shook his head in wonder.

He *loved* this place. It was a giant riddle.

Someone knocked. Expecting Pru or Mister Fox, he opened the door.

No one was there.

That's what ABE thought at first, anyway. A slight disturbance in the air alerted him to the presence of a *domovoi*. Squinting, ABE could barely make out the blurred shape of the telltale coat and hat. Apparently, the spirits were somewhat visible inside the Henhouse even without the looking glass.

The *domovoi* gestured, and its hands slipped out from beneath the sleeves of its coat. Unlike the rest of it, the *domovoi*'s hands showed clearly. Was it because they were the only part of its body not covered by clothing? Whether that was the case or not, ABE could see why Pru had seen nothing but the floating hands she had described on her first visit.

The spirit gestured again. Nodding his understanding, ABE exited his room. He closed the door and followed the seemingly disembodied hands. They traveled up through the Henhouse all the way to the attic, where a forest of branches reached from the floor to the top of the vaulted ceiling.

The effect gave the Henhouse a sort of visual logic

among its otherwise impossible architecture. It was as if all the tree trunk columns that separated the Henhouse's many levels crested in the attic, and he was walking through the canopy layer of that petrified forest.

As ABE ducked beneath a low-hanging branch, Pru's voice drifted back to him from somewhere up ahead.

"So he's okay?"

"He's fine. The *domovye* can't be killed," Mister Fox's voice answered.

They had to be talking about the *domovoi* ABE and Pru had seen vanish during its fight with the troll.

"They can, however, be weakened to the point where they disappear temporarily," Mister Fox added. "See, the *domovye* draw their strength from the Henhouse. The farther from it they roam, the weaker and less solid they become. If they go too far, or if they are injured, they lose their solid form and their essence returns to the Henhouse to regain its strength."

ABE rounded a branch and reached his destination. The *domovye* had set up a rectangular table in the middle of the Henhouse's forested interior. It was richly set with an assortment of silver platters and dishes. Mister Fox sat at one end and Pru sat at the other. Beyond them and through the trees, ABE could see the Henhouse's large circular window. Even in the distance, it seemed larger than he remembered.

ABE had read books about fairylands where mystical

beings spirited children away for magical feasts and celebrations. Looking around, he felt like he was a character in one of those stories.

In a way, he supposed he was.

"ABE," Pru greeted him. "It's about time. Come sit down. We're having pancakes."

An empty chair sat between her and Mister Fox. Up close, ABE saw that the place settings were all finely crafted and carved with intricate patterns. Smaller dishes of cream, assorted jams, and sliced salmon surrounded a large covered platter in the center of the table. There was also a bowl filled with what looked like small black beads.

A pained expression crossed Mister Fox's face. "We're not . . . Pru, I told you. They're not pancakes. They're blini, a traditional Russian breakfast."

"Whatever," Pru said as ABE took his seat. "But watch out for the black things, ABE. They're *fish eggs*. Gross, right?"

"It's called caviar, Pru. And I'll have you know it's considered a . . ." Mister Fox paused and tilted his head to one side.

Squinting, ABE saw a *domovoi* standing beside the detective, whispering in his ear.

"Excuse me a moment, you two. Let me deal with this." Mister Fox rose and walked a few feet away from the table to talk with the household spirit.

Pru leaned in toward ABE and whispered, "I actually knew they were called blini. He's said it like a dozen times already. He can be *such* a know-it-all. No offense."

"None taken—wait, what?" ABE stammered. He wasn't a know-it-all!

Was he?

No. He'd definitely know it if he was a know-it-all.

Mister Fox returned to the table. Before he could speak, Pru said, "Hey, ABE, remember how Mister Fox almost ran us over last night? You want to know why he did that? *Because he doesn't know how to drive!* Can you believe it?"

Mister Fox grimaced. "I've been traveling around in the Henhouse since I was younger than you are now. I'm sorry if I never learned how to drive a car. I'll tell you what. When *you* learn how to operate a magical house that travels about on a giant chicken foot, *then* you can be critical."

Pru stuck her tongue out at the detective. Since she had a mouth full of pancakes—or, rather, blini—the sight wasn't pretty.

"Very mature," Mister Fox said. He kind of gave up the moral high ground, though, because his mouth was also full as he spoke. Pru snickered.

"Let's get down to business. We have a lot on our plate," the detective said (after he'd swallowed). He held up a finger as ABE opened his mouth. "Just a figure of speech, ABE. I wasn't making a pun about breakfast."

Too bad. It would have been a good one.

"As I was about to say before Pru decided to comment on my driving, that *domovoi* was reporting back on things at Winterhaven House. In case you were wondering, everyone there is okay. Thor and Hilde fought off the trolls. Though apparently they did a fair amount of damage to the mansion."

"Do you know why they attacked?" Pru asked.

"No. But I don't like it. Their appearance on Midgard couldn't have been an accident. Someone must have sent them."

"Loki?" ABE asked.

Mister Fox frowned. "Possibly. But before we get into a conversation about Loki, I'd like to hear what you thought about yesterday's meeting."

"Well, I'm not excited about the whole end of the world thing," Pru said. "I kind of think we should do something about *that*."

"Fair point. But first, what were your impressions of the people there?"

"I was surprised by Odin," ABE said. "He seemed so . . . frail. I don't remember him being like that last year."

"Yeah," Pru agreed. "Me neither."

"That surprised me as well. I've heard things over the years suggesting that Odin had weakened since his visions of the future. The word is he sits on his high seat, alone, and watches events in the three worlds unfold. He doesn't participate. He doesn't interfere. He just sits and watches."

"It's kind of sad," ABE said. "He wasn't always like that. I mean, according to the stories, there was a time when Odin was almost like Prometheus."

"Who?" Pru asked.

"Sorry," ABE said. "Different set of myths. According to Greek myth, Prometheus was a Titan who stole fire from the gods and gave it to mortals."

"Odin gave fire to people?" Pru asked. "What was the point if this Prometheus guy had already done it?"

"No," Mister Fox said, taking up the story (which didn't seem *entirely* fair to ABE, who thought he'd been doing a fine job of telling it). "But there is an old story about how Odin snaked his way into a giant's stronghold and, taking the form of an eagle, flew off with something called the Mead of Poetry. He shared *that* with humankind. According to the story, the mead was a magical elixir that gave people the power of storytelling. Which, if you ask me, is at least as useful as fire."

"Odin changed into an eagle?" Pru asked. "He can shape-shift like Loki?"

"He can. It's a rare talent, but one that he and Loki

share. In fact, the two have a fair amount in common. They both have curious minds and prize intellect and knowledge. That's also uncommon among the Norse gods. You know that. You've met Thor. The point is, there was a time before Odin had his visions of the future when he and Loki were the best of friends. One of the tragedies of Ragnarok is that, according to the stories, they're destined to be generals on opposite sides.

"It was kind of hard to see him so weak yesterday," ABE said.

"Baldur's death really seems to have pushed him over the edge," Pru agreed.

"If so," Mister Fox said, "we might be able to make that work to our advantage. Given Odin's foreknowledge of events, he probably knows exactly where Loki is hiding. Odin could send Thor and Hilde right to him if he wanted to. But he seems inclined to let fate take its course and let the thunder god find Loki on his own. That gives us time to do our thing."

"Finally," Pru said. "Are you going to tell us now what 'our thing' is? What do we get to do?"

"Simple. While Thor and Hilde go on their quest to find Loki so they can punish him for killing Baldur, the three of us are going to launch an investigation into whether the trickster is actually guilty of the crime."

"WAIT." ABE SHOOK HIS HEAD IN DISBELIEF. "YOU WERE SERIOUS AT WINTER-haven House? You think Loki is *innocent*?"

"I never said that. All I said—all I'm *saying*—is that we don't know for sure whether he is innocent or guilty."

"You do remember Loki tried to kill ABE and me last year, right?" Pru asked.

"I'm not saying he's perfect," Mr. Fox admitted. "The question before us whether he committed *this* particular crime. If you—if *anyone*—can provide me with evidence that he did, then fine. Great. I will jump aboard the let's-catch-and-punish-Loki train. I'll even be the conductor. I'll wear a funny hat and everything."

"Another one?" Pru asked, smiling sweetly.

Mister Fox ignored her.

"The point is that there *isn't* any evidence. This is what we know. Baldur was killed during a feast at his home in Asgard. It was chaos. I had Ratatosk ask around. None of the gods saw what happened. There are even mixed reports on whether Loki was there. There's nothing to tie him to the murder except Odin's vision. The gods expect us to believe that vision without question. You two know my opinions on belief."

They did. One of the first things Mister Fox had said to them was that they shouldn't believe him. People believed too easily, according to him. Belief and certainty were what blinded people to magic. ABE suspected that one of the reasons Mister Fox nicknamed his detective agency the Unbelievable FIB—besides an understandable fondness for acronyms—was that a fib was something you shouldn't believe.

It made perfect sense that Mister Fox would want them to investigate Baldur's death and not just believe what they'd been told. Or, it *would* have made perfect sense if they were talking about anyone other than Loki.

It was easy for Mister Fox to try to be fair. He hadn't been kidnapped by Loki and handed over to Gristling. ABE had. And Gristling had threatened to do terrible things to him.

Terrible things.

There had been talk of bone grinding. And devouring.

That made it hard for ABE to be fair, or to give Loki the benefit of the doubt. He was sure Pru felt the same way. She would never agree with Mister Fox's plan.

"Okay," Pru said.

What?

"*Okay?*" ABE repeated, his voice rising in pitch. He cleared his throat and tried to speak normally. "You agree that Loki's innocent? Even after all he did to us last year? How come you're letting him off the hook so easy?"

"What can I say," Pru said, shrugging. "I have a forgiving nature."

"Since when?"

Pru narrowed her eyes and glared. "Careful, buddy, or I'll—"

"There!" ABE said, pointing at her. "See?"

Pru blushed and quickly recovered. She lifted her chin in the air primly. "I'm just *trying* to keep an open mind."

"That's all I ask," Mister Fox said. He had watched the exchange with his chin resting in one palm and his fingers covering his mouth. His hand didn't quite hide his smile.

ABE wasn't buying Pru's act. She was being far too reasonable. There had to be something else.

"So what are we looking for?" she continued.

"Motive and opportunity, right? We need to find out who had reason to kill Baldur, and who was in the right place at the right time to commit the crime. We'll need witnesses."

Of course. Pru loved being a detective. Investigating a murder mystery would be the holy grail of detective work to her.

Mister Fox nodded approvingly. "I couldn't have said it better myself. The gods are useless as witnesses. They were too distracted by their celebrations. But there were other people there at the scene of the crime—household servants. One of them must have seen something. You'll start there, with them."

ABE slumped in his chair. It looked like they'd be going on a mission to try to clear Loki's name, after all. He wished he felt better about the idea.

"I don't get it, though," he said with a sigh. "Wouldn't the easiest way to find out what happened to Baldur be to find Loki and ask him if he did it?"

"No," Mister Fox said. "Listen to me, both of you—this is important. We are *not* joining the search for Loki. I need you two to understand that. No matter what happens, no matter who tries to persuade you otherwise, you are *not* to go looking for Loki. Leave that quest to Thor and Hilde. Do you understand?"

"Fine with me," Pru said. She had a distant look in her eyes.

"ABE?" Mister Fox said.

ABE thought about it. Did he understand? He wasn't sure. Mister Fox was oddly insistent about them not joining the search for Loki. Why was that?

"If you say so," ABE said halfheartedly.

"Good," Mister Fox said. "Then tomorrow we'll start our investigation."

"Why tomorrow?" Pru asked. "Why not now?"

"I want Ratatosk to join you. He'll arrive tomorrow." Mister Fox grinned. He leaned back in his chair and clasped his hands behind his head. "It will be just like old times. What do you think? Are you both ready to become Fibbers again?"

"Please," Pru scoffed. "Like we ever stopped."

A short time later, ABE stood with Pru in front of the large circular window. While they waited for something—Mister Fox wouldn't say what—the detective explained the passage of time when traveling to and from Worlds of Myth. Behind them, back among the trees, dishes rattled as the *domovye* cleared the remains of breakfast from the table.

"Basically, time passes more slowly on Worlds of Myth than it does on Earth," Mister Fox said. "I could get into the mechanics of it more and talk about how Worlds of Myth are eternal realms where time, size, and distance are as much matters of perception as physics. But that complicates things. All you really need to know is that it doesn't matter how much time you spend on a World of Myth. The Henhouse will always be able to bring you home to the moment after you leave Earth."

Mister Fox was reassuring ABE, who had noticed during breakfast that the sky outside the Henhouse seemed to be getting darker—not brighter, as one would expect if it were morning. The detective had explained that they were on Asgard, not Earth, and that it was evening.

"So we don't have to worry about our parents missing us?" Pru asked.

"It shouldn't be an issue. ABE, the only reason you were gone overnight last year is because it took Pru and me a day to figure out where Loki had taken you."

They grew quiet after Mister Fox finished his explanation. ABE passed the time studying the window itself. It definitely seemed bigger. He asked Mister Fox about it.

"I might have misrepresented things a bit on your last visit when I described the Henhouse," the detective answered. "It's true that the Henhouse is a series of identical houses all occupying the same space. It's also true that each house is a slightly larger version of the one outside it. However, it's not true that the smallest version is the one you see on the outside or that this version we're standing in now is the largest. There are both smaller and larger versions. The Henhouse shows whatever side of her suits her mood."

"You fibbed," Pru said. "How surprising."

"I simplified things. You two had a lot to absorb."

Mister Fox's explanation seemed to confirm something ABE had been wondering about ever since the Henhouse in his room had started to glow. "The houses you gave us to hold our looking glasses aren't just models or copies of the Henhouse, are they?"

Mister Fox arched an eyebrow. "Very good. You're right. Those are smaller versions of the actual Henhouse that have been separated from the main building."

"So they're magic?" Pru asked.

"They are. How else do you think the *domovye* got to your houses so fast?"

"They came out of the Henhouses in our rooms?" ABE asked. But they were so small! Then again, size didn't seem to matter where the Henhouse was concerned.

"Of course," Mister Fox said. "All the versions of the Henhouse are connected. If necessary, the *domovye* can travel between them. Otherwise, they would have been too far from home to get to you two in time. As it was, their strength was diminished. Your Henhouses lost most of their magic when they were separated from the main one. Not all, but most. So the *domovye* were only operating at a fraction of their strength when they fought the troll. Usually, they're very strong."

"So how big is the Henhouse, really?" Pru asked.

"Honestly? I'm not sure. Sometimes at night I hear sounds that make me wonder if the *domovye* are still building. So I don't know how big . . . or how small . . . the Henhouse really is. Now shush. It's starting."

ABE turned to the window, curious about what Mister Fox had brought them to Asgard to see.

Outside, a line of figures carrying torches snaked its way through the darkness. Some of the figures broke off from the main group and lit a row of additional torches that must have been set out in preparation for whatever event was now taking place.

As the growing firelight brightened the scene, it revealed that the figures stood in a small bay framed by a rocky stretch of sand at one end and a high cliff at the other. The water reflected some of the torchlight, which also revealed a large, beached Viking longboat.

"How close are we?" ABE asked, surprised by how clearly he could see the people on the beach.

"Not as close as you'd think," Mister Fox said. "The oculus is magnifying the image."

"Oculus?" Pru asked.

"It's a word for an eye," ABE said. "Sometimes they call round openings in architecture an oculus, too."

"So it's the window? You could have just said it's the window, ABE."

"Sorry."

Mister Fox shushed them, and they resumed their observation of the events outside.

More figures moved into view below. They were carrying something. With a start, ABE realized it was a body. There were nine bearers. One was Thor. Odin trailed slightly behind the procession, stooped with exhaustion, age, or sorrow.

A phantom chill swept over ABE as he realized they were watching the funeral of the god Baldur.

The nine bearers and Odin continued to the edge of the water, where a long plank led up to the longboat. Still carrying Baldur's corpse, they climbed aboard. They laid Baldur on the deck and placed his shield and sword on top of him. Thor and the others stepped aside while Odin leaned down and lowered his head beside that of his dead son.

"What's he doing?" Pru asked.

"He's whispering something. No one knows what," Mister Fox said. "It's an odd detail that's survived in the myth about Baldur's death. The story clearly records that Odin whispers something into Baldur's ear. But nowhere is it written what Odin says. I've always wondered about that."

Odin rose and, taking a torch from Thor, touched it to Baldur's shroud. As the fire took hold, Thor held his hammer, Mjolnir, over the body of Baldur in a final salute or blessing. Then he and the others climbed off the boat.

Back on the shore, Thor and another figure ABE didn't recognize stepped forward and placed their shoulders against the stern of the vessel. Together, they pushed the ship into the water. As the lapping waves carried the longboat farther from shore, the fire of the funeral pyre burned higher and brighter. It became a pillar of light that illuminated the cliff face and revealed a host of figures perched atop the bluff. All bore silent witness to the final voyage of Baldur.

As the ship left the bay, the image in the oculus grew smaller, as though the window were a camera being pulled back. The pillar of light, bright though it had been, shrank to insignificance compared to the vast blackness of the open sea. The firelight no longer defied the darkness. All it did now was provide some scale to the overwhelming emptiness of the night. Soon the fire would burn out, and—with the death of Baldur's light—the dark would overwhelm the world.

CHAPTER 10

MISTER FOX PROVED AS GOOD AS HIS WORD. THE HENHOUSE RETURNED THE three travelers to Middleton at a time not long after they'd left. ABE and Pru walked home along the empty streets. Neither of them spoke much. The stark and solemn images of Baldur's funeral had touched them both, though ABE thought it had been harder for Pru. It must have reminded her of her dad's funeral. He tried to think of something to say, but nothing seemed enough. He hadn't lost anyone, not like she had. The difference in their experiences wasn't a gap—it was a chasm, and he had no idea how to cross it. So he just walked along beside her.

It was still dark out as ABE slipped back inside his house and climbed the stairs to his room. He didn't think he would sleep. After all, he'd already eaten breakfast. But his trips to the Henhouse and to Asgard had messed with his sense of the day, and the darkness outside his window whispered to him that it was still time to doze. He lay on his bed and, before he knew it, drifted off.

The dream came quickly.

He stood in a forest. Only, it wasn't a proper forest. The trees that rose up around him weren't trees at all but a complex network of roots that stretched down from the sky. The roots belonged to Yggdrasil, the giant ash tree that connected the three worlds of Norse mythology. ABE was in Asgard, the place where Loki had brought him to recover the Eye of Odin.

He had read an article once that there was no such thing as a recurring dream. According to the article, the notion of a repeated dream was a trick of memory, like déjà vu. ABE didn't think he believed that. He *knew* this dream. It had haunted him for a year.

Usually, the events of the dream followed what he remembered from his abduction. In it, he relived his trip to Asgard with Pru and Ratatosk. Only he was never as lucky in his dream as they had been in real life. The dream always ended with Gristling reaching for him, a wicked leer on his face.

This time, though, the familiar dream took an unexpected turn.

A wall of mist rolled through the dreamscape like a tidal wave. It erased the familiar surroundings and replaced everything with a sea of undulating gray. Only the roots remained visible—except they no longer resembled trees. They looked more like bars that imprisoned him.

Panic gripped him. He tried to run to the tree line so he could escape the bars that now formed a circle around him, like a cage. But the mist was cold and unnaturally thick. Moving through it was like swimming through jelly.

A flicker of movement to his left drew his attention. He tried to turn to get a better look at the disturbance, but the mist slowed his movements. By the time he'd turned, whatever had been there was gone.

Another flash of motion caught his eye, this time to his right and a little bit closer. He struggled to turn more quickly. He managed to get a quick glimpse of a woman before she disappeared into a thicker patch of rising mist. She wore a black cowl with the hood pulled up over her head.

The temperature plummeted. ABE pulled his hands up into his sleeves and hugged his arms to his chest in an effort to stay warm as the cold stabbed at his skin like tiny needles.

The woman appeared again. ABE didn't have to turn to see her. She strode into view directly ahead of him on the other side of the roots, and this time he saw her clearly.

Hair the color of a freshly dug grave spilled over her left shoulder in long tendrils that curled like worms on the pavement after a storm. She held the right side of her hood tightly in one hand, concealing that half of her face. Her one visible eye bore into him.

ABE opened his mouth to ask who she was. Before he could speak, though, she turned quickly and began to walk away from him. The mist rose up once more and stole her from his sight.

Nothing happened for what seemed like a long time. Just as ABE began to worry that he would be stuck there in the limbo of his dream forever, a voice drifted through the mist. It was a woman's voice. It came from everywhere and nowhere at once.

"I carry a riddle for you, young hero, a message from another. Listen. *When is a truth-teller not telling the truth?*"

ABE blinked in surprise.

A riddle?

Young hero?

Before he could answer (not that he even had an answer!), the mist retreated. It fled as if someone had hit a rewind button and reversed the tidal wave that had brought the fog in the first place.

Within seconds, ABE found his dream had returned

him once more to the roots of Yggdrasil in Asgard. But he wasn't alone. He staggered back as he found himself face-to-face with the giant Gristling. The monster grinned and reached for him.

ABE woke up screaming. He sat up and fumbled for his light. A flurry of movement by his window temporarily distracted him. When he managed to switch on his bedside lamp, though, he found his room empty. The curtains billowed slightly in a breeze. He hadn't realized he'd left his window open.

ABE collapsed back onto his bed. Afterimages of the nightmare drifted though his mind. He saw the hauntingly beautiful woman when he closed his eyes. Her voice—he assumed it was her voice, anyway—echoed through his thoughts: *When is a truth-teller not telling the truth?*

It was a strange sort of question.

Even stranger was the answer that occurred to ABE.

He repeated the question out loud. "When is a truth-teller not telling the truth?"

He couldn't quite bring himself to say the answer out loud, though. It made him uncomfortable, as if he was being disloyal to a friend. So he whispered the answer in his head: *When he's a Fibber.*

CHAPTER 11

"I CAN'T BELIEVE IT'S THE FIRST DAY OF SCHOOL ALREADY," PRU SAID TO ABE the next morning in homeroom. "You wouldn't believe the nightmare I had last night after we got home."

A wave of relief washed over ABE. He'd been worrying about his own nightmare ever since he woke up. The whole thing had seemed so weird and vivid and alien that it had almost felt like a dream that someone else had imagined and then stuck in his head.

That sounded crazy. He knew it. But if Pru had dreamt something similar, then maybe there *had* been something unnatural about the dream after all.

"Really?" he said. "I'm kind of glad to hear that."

"I dreamt that Mr. Jeffries got up in front of the

class and then reached under the collar of his shirt and *pulled off his face*—except it wasn't his face. It was a mask! And underneath was Mrs. Edleman! She just looked at me and said, 'I'm ba-aaack.'"

"Oh."

"I *know.* Pretty awful, right?"

"Uh, yeah. That does sound pretty bad."

"Tell me about it. I bet you didn't have any nightmares about the first day of school."

"Um, no," ABE said. "Not about that."

"Of course not. You love school. You're the only kid I know who looks forward to the school year starting."

"I never said I was looking forward to school."

"ABE, come on. You're sniffing your notebook as we speak."

"What? I am not . . . Oh." ABE lowered his notebook with its fresh, soothing bouquet of newly opened loose-leaf paper. Changing the subject, he said, "You're in a good mood, all things considered."

"I *am* bummed about summer vacation being over, obviously."

"Right. But, no . . . I kind of meant the possible end of the world."

Pru glanced around to make sure no one was paying attention to their conversation. She needn't have worried. The other kids in homeroom were fist-bumping and high-fiving as though they hadn't seen each other for months, which was odd since Middleton was so small you couldn't turn around without seeing some-one you knew.

"Well, there's that," Pru said. "But I guess I'm *not* too worried about Ragnarok. I know I should be. Maybe part of me is. But, ABE, Mister Fox is *back*. He'll fix things. I know he will."

"You really believe in him, don't you?"

"Of course I do. But don't you dare tell him that!"

ABE looked down at his feet. His new shoes had brought him very little comfort so far that morning.

Obviously, Pru believed in Mister Fox. She *should* believe in him. ABE should, too. There had been a time after they'd first met the detective that ABE hadn't believed in him. But he had moved past that. Hadn't he?

So how come his dreams told him that Mister Fox was lying to them?

"Are you okay?" Pru asked, studying him. "You're being quieter than usual."

"Yeah. I guess . . . I guess I'm just having trou-ble with this whole idea of thinking about Loki as innocent."

"Oh," Pru said, sounding satisfied with ABE's re-sponse. "That. Well, I understand that. But an inves-tigation is an investigation. As long as it means we get to go on another adventure, I'm willing to play along.

And imagine if we get to prove Mister Fox is wrong. Think about how much fun *that* could be."

ABE couldn't help smiling at her as Mr. Jeffries stepped to the front of the room.

"So. First day of school," he said, "Always a strange thing, am I right? New room. New teachers. I'm sure you're all wondering what to make of me. I'll tell you what I make of myself. I like to think that I'm fair. Which means that if you try your best and treat each other—and me—with respect, then there's a good chance you'll survive homeroom and language arts. After that, no promises. Junior high is its own world, am I right?"

A few of the kids chuckled. Even Pru smiled a bit. ABE couldn't remember her ever laughing at one of Mrs. Edleman's jokes.

Then again, he couldn't remember Mrs. Edleman ever actually making a joke. So maybe it wasn't a fair comparison.

"Let's get things started," Mr. Jeffries continued. "First of all, in just a moment I'm going to ask everyone to walk over to the carpeted area in the front of the room and sit down in a circle.

"No, seriously?"

ABE looked over at the boy who had spoken. He recognized the kid as the same one who had laughed at him the night of the open house. According to Pru, his name was Danny. He'd been in the other sixth-grade class last year. Pru described him as one of those kids who was nice to your face—but only to your face.

"Seriously," Mr. Jeffries said. He addressed the whole room with his next words. "I get it. Sitting together in a circle to start the day sounds babyish, right? I know it will take some getting used to. If it makes you feel any better, classes all the way through twelfth grade started their day this way at the school where I used to teach. The idea is that it builds a sense of community. You'll all be going from one class to the next this year. It can get kind of hectic. Call me corny, but I want you to think of this as your *home*room, not just in name."

It did sound corny. It also sounded kind of nice.

Pru seemed to think so, too. She sat up straighter, and ABE could tell she was making an effort to look interested in what Mr. Jeffries was saying.

"I'd call it corny, all right," Danny said, quietly enough that his voice wouldn't carry to the front of the room. "And lame."

"Be quiet, Danny," Pru said. "It's his first day, too."

ABE wiggled a finger in his ear. Had he heard that right? Had Pru just defended a teacher?

At the front of the room, Mr. Jeffries cleared his throat. His tone was friendly but firm as he said, "One of the things that you'll all quickly learn about me is that I'm a fan of courtesy. When it's your turn to talk, I'll listen. I promise. Just keep in mind that I expect the same in return."

Though his words were addressed to the whole class, his eyes settled on Pru as he finished talking. A slight frown crossed his face. It was quick. ABE wanted to think he'd imagined it. But as Pru sank red-faced into her chair, it was clear that she had noticed it, too.

PRU AND ABE WENT TO THE HENHOUSE AS SOON AS SCHOOL ENDED. As so often seemed the case with first days of school, the afternoon felt particularly fall-like. The first stains of yellow and orange showed among the green leaves.

"Little house, little house, hear my plea. Turn from the woods and look at me," Pru said as they reached the ramshackle hut that served as the headquarters of the Unbelievable FIB.

ABE took a step back as the Henhouse stood up. With an ease that one might not normally expect from a house balanced on a single chicken leg, the Henhouse made a full rotation. Planks of wood shifted and the sound of feathers rustling filled the air.

When the Henhouse settled again, an arched double door stood in front of them atop rickety steps. The oculus looked out at them from above.

"Here we go!" Pru said as she pushed open the doors.

Again thinking about his dream, ABE wasn't paying attention to his surroundings as he entered. So he nearly ran right into Pru where she'd stopped, just a few yards in.

The hallway had ended. Before them was a small but cozy sitting room. Dark wood paneling covered the walls, but the space was brightened by art that hung in frames throughout the small room. The paintings and drawings depicted fantastic landscapes and impossible creatures. They all appeared to have been done by the same artist.

Mister Fox sat in one of three overstuffed chairs in the center of the room. He looked up to greet them as they entered. "Welcome."

"What happened?" Pru asked. Then, in an accusing voice, she added, "Where's the rest of the Henhouse? Did you break it?"

"Don't be ridiculous. You can't *break* the Henhouse." Mister Fox hesitated, then added, "Well, okay, technically you can. And I did. Once. But that was a long time ago. Everything is fine now. No, I just convinced the *domovye* to rearrange things a bit for your visit. You won't be staying long, so I figured I'd save you a climb to the oculus and meet you here, in one of the smaller versions of the Henhouse. That way, we can chat briefly and then have you off on your investigation."

"What do you want to talk about?" Pru asked, sitting in one of the two remaining chairs.

"Assumptions."

"What about them?" ABE asked, also taking a seat.

"I'll tell you one of the hardest parts about being a Fibber and investigating mysteries that involve mythical beings. We tend to think we know the individuals we're dealing with because we know the myths. That's a dangerous assumption."

"Does this have something to do with what you said once about stories changing over time?" Pru asked.

"In part. Stories exist at the whim of the teller. Myths have been told over and over again. So, yes, we have to take the details in them with a grain of salt. But there's more to think about than that."

"Like what?" ABE asked.

"The Mythics themselves. The temptation is to see them through the lens of the stories you know. But the thing about stories, especially old ones—and most especially myths—is that they reduce characters to their most basic elements. That's where archetypes come from."

"What's an archetype?" Pru asked. She squeezed her eyes shut as soon as the question was out, perhaps realizing she'd opened the door to another visit from ABE-the-walking-dictionary.

ABE didn't disappoint. *Not* because he was a know-it-all. It was just good information to have.

"It's a type of character that you see over and over again in stories. The trickster figure is a good example. Loki is the trickster in the Norse myths, but there are tricksters in other myths from around the world, too. They're all kind of different, but also kind of the same."

"How so?" Pru asked. She sounded reluctantly interested.

"Well, trickster figures all share some common traits. They're usually able to change their shape, for example. They're also usually greedy. That greed can drive them to cause trouble, but sometimes their actions can bring about good things and be a boon to people, too. Like Thor wouldn't have a hammer if it wasn't for one of Loki's pranks."

"The funny part," Mister Fox added, "is that Mythics have taken a liking to humankind's terms, like *trickster*. Mythics use those words, too. But the point is that archetypes can be misleading. If we think we know a Mythic because we know the myth, then we risk overlooking important truths.

"Mythics are just like us. They're complicated.

They have desires and fears and hopes. That's why I wanted you to see Baldur's funeral. I want you to remember that these are real people. The myths don't always capture that."

"So basically you want us to keep an open mind when we're talking to people in Asgard," ABE said.

"Interrogating witnesses," Pru corrected.

"Exactly," Mister Fox agreed. "In the past, I've told you that Fibbers ask questions and seek answers. In other words, I've told you to be suspicious of other people's truths. Now I'm telling you that you should be suspicious of your *own* truths—or things you think are true. In short, avoid assumptions. They're just beliefs in different clothes."

"This is about you still thinking that Loki is innocent, isn't it?" ABE asked. He couldn't quite keep the resentment from his voice.

"This is about me thinking that we should go into this investigation without assuming we know how it will end," Mister Fox said. He peered at ABE. "I thought we were on the same page with that."

ABE ducked his head. "I know. It's just . . . never mind."

"Just what, ABE?" Mister Fox asked.

ABE couldn't bring himself to look at the detective. He couldn't just ignore the question, though.

"It's nothing. Forget it. I just had a weird dream last night. It really shook me up. I'll get over it."

"Is that all?" Pru asked. She rolled her eyes.

But Mister Fox leaned forward in his chair, his full attention on ABE.

"Dream? What kind of dream?"

"A nightmare, really," ABE said.

"Is that right?" Mister Fox sat back. His nose twitched. "I think you'd better tell us about it, ABE. Try not to leave anything out."

ABE took a deep breath. He told them about the woman and her riddle. He tried to convey what a *strange* dream it had been.

"Okay," Pru said when he finished. "I admit that sounds like a weird nightmare. But I don't see why it's got you so shook up. It's just a dream."

"He's shook up because he doesn't really think it *was* just a dream. He thinks it was a message, like it claimed. Isn't that right, ABE?"

"That sounds crazy, doesn't it?"

"Pretty much," Pru said.

The detective shushed her. "No, ABE. It doesn't sound crazy. Well, I don't think so, anyway. And I'm the one you should be listening to just now."

ABE looked away again.

"Ah . . . I see." Understanding dawned on the

detective's face. "That's the problem, isn't it? You're not sure you *can* trust me at the moment, are you?"

"Why wouldn't he trust you?" Pru asked, as ABE slouched deeper into his chair. "That's nuts."

"Easy, Pru. There was a time you doubted me, too. I seem to remember a particular incident involving you trying to set my house on fire."

"Why does everyone keep bringing that up?" Pru demanded. "*Once*. I tried to set your house on fire once. *People make mistakes.* Seriously, you guys have to get over it. Besides, we're talking about ABE. Why doesn't he trust you?"

"He thinks the riddle might be about me. Is that it, ABE? Are you worried I'm lying to you about something?"

ABE wished he could disappear into his chair. Mister Fox's sympathetic tone only made him feel worse. The detective was defending him!

"No . . . Maybe. I don't know. Loki did so many terrible things last year. And you seem so eager to let him off the hook! Then I had that dream: 'When is a truth-teller not telling the truth?' I thought . . ."

"You thought the answer was 'When he's a Fibber,'" Mister Fox said. "You thought the dream was warning you about me. I understand, ABE. It makes sense."

"No," Pru said. She looked at ABE. "It doesn't.

First of all, Mister Fox *isn't* a Fibber. That's what he calls the kids he works with. Which means even if your solution *is* right, it's more likely the riddle is talking about one of us. And how do you know the answer is a *he*? Maybe it's 'When *she's* a Fibber.'"

"Oh!" ABE said. "I . . . I hadn't thought about it like that."

"So," Pru added, arching her eyebrows, "are *you* lying about anything, ABE?"

"No!"

"Good. Because I'm not, either." Pru tilted her head to the side. "Well, not about anything I can think of at the moment, anyway."

ABE buried his face in his hands. What had he been thinking? He'd let a dream make him doubt a friend. He forced himself to look the detective in the eye.

"Mister Fox, I'm so sorry. Really. I shouldn't have doubted you. I guess I really am just having a hard time keeping an open mind about Loki. I was kind of upset that you were willing to forgive him for all he did and—"

"ABE, stop. You have nothing to apologize for. You only did what I've always encouraged you to do. You questioned things. And, for all we know, the riddle could still be about me."

"Wait," Pru said. "You mean you *are* lying to us?"

"Not about anything big," the detective said with

a wink. "But that's not the point. The riddle doesn't directly suggest *lying*. Someone could not be telling the truth because they don't know what the truth is. They could be wrong, and therefore what they're saying *wouldn't* be true. But the meaning of the message doesn't concern me much at the moment. I'm more curious about who sent it."

"Any ideas?" Pru asked.

"One or two. But I want to do some research. We'll discuss it when you get back. One last thing before you go, though." The detective reached out and put a hand on ABE's shoulder. "You're wrong, ABE. I haven't forgiven Loki for what he did to you or Pru last year. Not by a long shot. But this investigation is bigger than that. If Loki *is* innocent and we can prove it, then maybe Ragnarok doesn't have to happen, ever. Maybe all those people don't have to die. I think that's worth exploring. Don't you?"

"Yeah," ABE said with a grateful nod. "I do."

MISTER FOX HAD A GIFT FOR THEM BEFORE THEY LEFT.

"Clothes?" Pru said, examining the pile of items a *domovoi* handed to her. "Clothes are the worst kind of gift."

"These are special clothes. They'll help you fit in on Asgard."

"I didn't have special clothes last year when I rescued ABE."

"You were trying to remain unnoticeable last time. This time is different. This time we want people in Asgard to notice you. We want them to talk to you. These will help."

ABE looked down at the folded clothes Mister Fox

had provided. There was a pair of sturdy brown pants and a blue long-sleeved shirt. Both items looked like something that might have been worn in a Viking village hundreds of years ago.

"Where did you get them?" he asked.

"The *domovye* made them. They have many talents, but domestic magic is their specialty. They're particularly good with fabric. They make their own clothes, which render them almost invisible. Your clothes will do the opposite. The *domovye* have enchanted them, so they'll make you *more* visible. People will be able to see and interact with you."

Mister Fox and Pru stepped out into the hallway while ABE changed. Then ABE and Pru switched. Pru came out wearing clothes that looked a lot like ABE's, only her shirt was green, with a different pattern embroidered around the neck. She also carried a satchel over her shoulder, presumably provided to replace her messenger bag. Mister Fox had been smart to include it. Pru kept her dad's detective badge in her messenger bag. She'd carried the badge with her ever since his death. She'd told ABE that carrying the badge was like carrying a piece of her dad with her. She didn't go *anywhere* without it. ABE guessed the badge and her looking glass had already been transferred to the satchel.

The detective walked them down the hall but held back as they approached the exit.

"This is as far as I go. The rest is up to you two. Go to Baldur's house and find out what you can. Then come back. Hurry, now. There's someone outside who's been waiting to see you both."

*

The Henhouse had settled on a hilltop. A short distance away, beyond a massive wall, stood the city of Asgard. Magnificent buildings rose from the ground, monuments of timber and stone. Their multilayered and peaked roofs stretched toward the sky and glistened in the sun.

ABE had read that the dwarves that lived in the nearby mountains provided the gods with a wealth of jewels and precious stones. He suspected those gems decorated the buildings and were catching the light, causing the sparkle.

"So that's Asgard," ABE said from the steps. "It's . . . amazing."

Before Pru could answer, a small, furry projectile launched itself at her from the roof of the Henhouse. Her cries of "What is it?" and "Get it off!" quickly stopped when she realized the newcomer's identity.

"Ratatosk!" she exclaimed

"Shortwits!" Ratatosk answered.

ABE wasn't offended by the greeting—well, not too much. It was the squirrel's way. He'd spent a lifetime carrying insults back and forth between the eagle that lived at the top of Yggdrasil and the dragon, Nidhogg, who lived at the bottom. They'd sort of been a bad influence on Ratatosk's language development. And his social development. Still, Ratatosk did seem very pleased to see them, despite his greeting. He scampered up to Pru's shoulder and nuzzled her cheek before head-butting ABE's shoulder.

"It's so good to see you," ABE said.

"Yeah," Pru agreed. "But how come you never came to visit us?"

"Has it been long? It's so hard to tell with you mortals. You hurry through days so fast! Rush, rush, rush! It can't have been *that* long, no. You're still relatively *short* shortwits."

"What? Look who's talking!" Pru said. "You don't even come up to my knee."

Ratatosk sniffed. "I'm very big for a squirrel, yes! Tall. Stately. Statuesque!"

"So," ABE said, clearing his throat, "this is Asgard, huh? We were just saying how fantastic it is."

"Yes, yes, yes. Splendid Asgard, home of the apotheosized gods and their overblown egos."

"Apo . . . theo . . . sized?" Pru repeated.

"Glorified," ABE said.

Ratatosk huffed, as though he had wanted to explain.

"Sorry," ABE said.

Pru shook her head at the both of them. "If you two could stop trying to impress each other with your *apotheosized* vocabularies for a second, that would be great. This is my first Mythic city. I'm trying to have a moment."

"Sorry," ABE said as Ratatosk snorted.

Pru laughed and ABE did, too, struck by the pleasure of the reunion and familiar roles. Ratatosk soon joined the laughter. ABE assumed Ratatosk's quick breathing was what passed as laughter for the squirrel, anyway.

"We should get going," Pru said as they quieted. "Ratatosk, can you take us to Baldur's house?"

The squirrel nodded, and the three of them set off down the hill toward the gates of Asgard. Pru glanced back at the Henhouse.

"He'll be okay," ABE said. He hoped that was true. "I'm sure he's used to this by now."

"I know. But . . . this place, ABE. Breathe it in. Like you said, it's *amazing*. We're in a whole other world. Imagine being able to travel to places like this all your life . . . and then suddenly not being able to go anymore."

ABE nodded, not knowing what to say. He hadn't been sure how he would react to a return to Asgard. His first trip had been terrifying. This time, though, ABE felt an excited quiver in his belly as he approached the fabled city.

In a way, visiting Asgard was like traveling back in time. The view of the city from the hilltop had revealed a metropolis that resembled drawings ABE had seen of a Viking village, though on a much, much grander scale. He might as well have been stepping into one of his favorite books as they approached the gates and the smell of fish and smoked meat filled the air while the clanging of metal rang in the distance.

Ratatosk slipped into Pru's bag as they passed through the gates, huge wooden doors tall enough to give even the giant Gristling pause.

"I have a bit of a reputation," the squirrel explained. "Best if I stay out of sight, yes."

"Maybe if you didn't insult people so often, you'd have a better reputation," Pru said.

Ratatosk snorted.

"Where did all the people come from?" ABE asked as they walked the crowded streets. The stories mostly talked about Asgard as the home of the gods and goddesses. But Asgard was filled with people.

"There are three classes in Asgard," Ratatosk explained from Pru's bag. "The gods and goddesses are one. Haughty. Imperious. Warriors are next. Most are mortals that Odin and the Valkyries brought here to live in Valhalla and train, waiting for Ragnarok. They fight and eat, eat and fight. An army of barbarous gluttons. They die each night to rise the next day and fight some more."

"Some life," Pru said.

"Who said they were alive? Not alive, no. Not dead. Something in between."

"What's the last group?" ABE asked, shivering at the thought of the undead warriors.

"Serfs. When the worlds started to drift apart, the gods allowed some mortals to come here to live and serve them. Why be a god if there is no one to worship you?"

"Those must be the people Mister Fox wants us to talk to at Baldur's house."

Ahead, a large timber building loomed over them. ABE couldn't quite figure out how many stories it was. It seemed to be a mass of sloping roofs that intersected with each other at various stages. Braided carvings trimmed the wood.

A strange feeling settled over ABE as they approached the building.

"It feels so . . ." he struggled for the right word.

"Peaceful," Pru said, finishing his thought.

"That is Breidablik," another voice said.

ABE turned to see a girl in a long dress approach from around a corner of the building. She appeared to be a few years younger than them.

"What is?" Pru said, looking around.

"That feeling." The girl laughed. "That sense of peace you feel. It comes from Breidablik, home of Baldur, fairest of the gods. Welcome."

CHAPTER 14

"IS THIS YOUR FIRST TIME IN THE SHINING CITY?" THE GIRL ASKED. "HAVE you come from far away?"

"You could say that," Pru said.

"I have heard of other villages, but I have not been to any! I am Eira." The girl ducked her head in a greeting. "My mother is Alva. She is . . . *was* a weaver here at Breidablik. She left after . . . what happened. She couldn't stand to be here anymore."

"Eira!" a voice called from inside the building. "Quickly, now! No dawdling."

"I must go!" Eira said.

"Wait," Pru said. "We want to ask you about . . ." Her voice trailed off as Eira rushed off and disappeared into the building.

"Well, at least we know we're in the right place," ABE said as they followed the girl into Breidablik.

Baldur's home welcomed them with its vast halls, open courtyards, and sprawling gardens. They wandered aimlessly, not sure where to start or whom they should ask about Baldur's death. In the end, because they encountered so few people after Eira, they asked anyone they could.

The first person they met was a gray-bearded old man. He walked with a stoop and a head turned slightly to one side, as though he had spent a good deal of time bent over things and never quite got the hang of straightening back up again.

"Hello, children," he said cheerfully. He introduced himself as Harald and explained he was a tanner.

"I'm Pru. This is my friend ABE. Nice to meet you. You know, we were starting to think we were the only ones here. You're only the second person we've seen. Where is everyone?"

"Oh, there are few enough of us left here now—that's a fact," Harald said, scratching his beard with calloused fingers. "Since our poor master died, there's little call for work."

"Yeah, we heard about Baldur," Pru said, jumping at the opening. She shook her head. "Terrible news. Did you . . . by any chance see what happened?"

"No, no. I was on an errand and away."

"But you must have heard about it, right?" Pru pressed.

"Who would talk about such a thing? Who would bring such bad fortune on themselves?" Harald asked, blinking. Then, perhaps realizing that he himself was talking about it, he looked around anxiously. "I must be off. Good day, children. Be well. Enjoy the peace of Breidablik."

Harald hurried off.

"That didn't go so well," ABE observed.

"You think?"

Their luck didn't change as the day went on. The few cooks and groundskeepers they met were friendly enough at first. But everyone ran off as soon as ABE or Pru mentioned Baldur or Loki.

"This is getting us nowhere!" Pru complained. "What's wrong with these people? How am I supposed to interrogate anyone if they won't answer my questions?"

"Serfs are a superstitious lot," Ratatosk said. "*Over*-credulous, yes. *Un*skeptical. They know Baldur's death heralds dark days ahead."

"At least people are friendly," ABE said.

"Yeah," Pru said. "Why is that? I mean, we're just wandering around in here. How come nobody is throwing us out?"

"I've been wondering about that, too. Remember what the girl said about Breidablik being peaceful?

That kind of fits with some of the things I read about the place. The stories say nothing unclean can enter its walls. It's supposed to be a safe haven. I think the people here are used to an open-door policy."

"Yes, yes," Ratatosk said from inside the bag. "Odin placed a charm on Breidablik to keep anyone with evil intent from entering. Guests are allowed to walk freely."

"Speaking of evil intent," Pru said, gesturing down the hall in which they stood. "I think we're being watched."

ABE looked. Eira's head poked out from around a corner a short distance away. Discovered, the girl approached them, blushing.

"I'm sorry. I did not mean to listen in," she said.

"No harm in a little eavesdropping," Pru said with a shrug.

"In that case, may I ask a question? Did your bag just talk a moment ago?"

ABE exchanged a look with Pru. She raised her eyebrows. He shrugged. What did they have to lose? They weren't getting anywhere on their own. Maybe Ratatosk could help.

"Okay, I'll show you," Pru said. "But it's a secret. Okay?"

Eira nodded eagerly and Pru opened her bag. The girl peered inside. Ratatosk winked at her and waved. Eira jumped back, clapping a hand over her mouth.

"The Messenger!" she said, her fingers muffling her voice. "Who *are* you that you travel with the Messenger?"

ABE didn't want to lie to Eira. He also knew they couldn't tell her the truth. He and Pru had to fit in by appearing as though they belonged, the way Odin did when he masqueraded as Old Man Grimnir.

"Pru and I are, um, apprenticed to a storyteller." That was sort of true, he supposed. They were kind of apprenticed to Mister Fox. And a fibber was someone who told stories, after all.

"You're skalds? But why are you here? And how is it you travel with the Messenger? Are you friends of the gods?"

"We are," Pru said. "Totally. They sent us to gather information for a new story about Baldur's death."

ABE nodded, impressed with how quickly Pru had adapted to his story and improved on it. They hadn't had any luck just asking people about Baldur's death. But maybe Eira would be more talkative if she thought they were creating a story for the gods.

"Were you here when it happened . . . when Baldur died?" Pru asked. ABE held his breath as he waited for an answer.

"No," Eira said, and ABE's shoulders drooped. "But my mother was here that day. You could come with me to my house tonight! My mother would be so pleased to have skalds who know the gods under her roof. I'm sure she will do whatever she can to help you!"

*

The sun hung low in the sky as ABE and Pru arrived at Eira's village just outside the walls of Asgard. It consisted of a collection of about twenty long, rectangular houses. The walls of the houses were made with stacked logs. They reminded ABE of building toys he'd had when he was little.

They followed Eira along the worn paths that marked the roads of the village. Around them, people lit torches and lanterns as the dark began to gather. Everyone ABE saw cast frequent looks over their shoulders and spoke in hushed tones.

Eira's home looked like all the other buildings. The door stood in the center of one of the long walls of the house. Tears welled in ABE's eyes as he entered the smoke-filled interior. At first, he worried the house had caught fire. But as his eyes stopped watering, he realized the space just lacked ventilation for the long, open hearth located in the center of the structure's only room.

A woman sat beside the fire, tending a large iron cauldron that hung on a chain from a roof beam. Eira introduced her as her mother, Alva.

"Mother, this is ABE and, er, Pru," Eira said, stumbling a bit over their names. "I met them at Breidablik. They're skalds!"

Eira's mother snorted and said, "A bit young for skalds."

"But, Mother," Eira said, "they travel with—"

"Apprentice skalds," Pru interrupted, elbowing Eira. ABE leaned in to remind the girl that Ratatosk was a secret.

"We're gathering information about the death of Baldur for a story—" Pru continued.

"Hush, child! We do not speak of that in this house," Alva said, rising to her feet and wiping her hands on her apron. "Eira, go fetch your brother. Your friends may stay for dinner, but we will have no gossip under this roof."

"Okay. Not a promising start," Pru whispered to ABE as Eira followed her mother's directions. "But I'll wear her down. Adults are easy. Watch. It's just a matter of coming at it from the right angle."

Eira returned with her brother, Sten, and the family sat down for a meal of fish and some drink that ABE was pretty sure his mom wouldn't have let him try at home. Pru began her interrogation as soon as dinner started.

"Beautiful weather, wouldn't you say? I bet it was a dark day when Baldur died."

"Weather?" Alva said. "Who can attend to the weather when there is work to be done? Most days I don't know if the sun shines or the snow falls."

Pru chewed her lip. ABE made a note to slip the definition of *subtle* into a conversation with Pru. Soon.

"That's a beautiful dress, though," Pru said later. "Was that what you wore the day Baldur died?"

"Clothes! Don't talk to me about clothes. I have baskets of clothing to mend for my own children and others in the village. I hardly notice my own clothes. For all I know, I might have gone naked to Breidablik that day."

Sten and Eira giggled. Pru's bottom lip was beginning to chap from all the lip-chewing Alva's evasions had inspired.

When the meal was done, Sten asked ABE and Pru for a story. Alva sat back expectantly. Apparently, being an apprentice skald—even a pretend one—came with certain obligations.

ABE figured the task would fall to him. Pru surprised him, though, by rising to her feet first.

"Listen now to the story of the Eye of Odin," she said. "It begins in the land of Midgard, across the Rainbow Bridge. There, in a small town, there lived a brave young girl who was not at all small for her age. Her name was Prudence the Red. Prudence had a loyal friend named Aloysius the Fierce and a magical pet fox who she called Mister Fox."

ABE groaned. Pru ignored him and continued.

"Now, it just so happened that, long ago, Odin, Allfather of the gods, had hidden a very special stone in

Prudence's town. On that stone was written the secret location of the Eye of Odin, a magical talisman that had the power to see into the very future."

"Ooh," exclaimed Sten and Eira at once. Even Alva appeared caught up in Pru's telling.

Just then, a different voice reached ABE's ears. It came from Pru's bag. But it wasn't Ratatosk's voice. It was Mister Fox, trying to reach them through the looking glass.

Before ABE could react, Ratatosk peeked out, unnoticed, and grabbed a nearby piece of cloth. He pulled it into the bag and must have wrapped the glass in it because Mister Fox's voice became muffled and then fell silent. ABE followed Ratatosk's lead and quietly wrapped his own glass with a napkin, then stuffed it in the bag.

Pru went on to tell how the brave band of heroes journeyed to Asgard and temporarily recovered the Eye of Odin, only to lose it once again to Loki. ABE had to admit that Pru was a talented storyteller. Even having lived through the events, ABE found himself caught up in her telling as they reached the moment when Prudence the Red, Aloysius the Fierce, and Ratatosk were cornered by Gristling and Loki and about to meet their end.

"But Prudence the Red knew just what to do," Pru said. "Do you know why?"

"Because she was very brave and very smart?" Eira asked, her eyes wide.

"Well, yes. That. Definitely that. But also because when she had held the Eye, even though it was only for a short time, *she had seen the future*. She knew just what to do to save herself and her friends. She took a deep breath and called for her close, personal friend, Thor. *BOOM!* He arrived in an explosion of thunder, and there was a huge battle. Thor polished off the giants, and then they hid the Eye of Odin once again so Loki would never, ever find it!"

Eira and Sten cheered. And, a bit to ABE's surprise, Alva joined in.

"I have a question, though," Sten said. "What did Mister Fox do?"

"Surprisingly little," Pru said. She was really enjoying the authority of being the storyteller. "Mostly, he got in the way and made sarcastic remarks. But Prudence the Red was generous and kept him around anyway."

"Oh."

"It was a fine story," Alva said. "You more than earned your meal and a night's lodging."

"A night's lodging?" ABE said. "That's nice. But we can't stay."

"You certainly can't go!" Alva said.

"Oh, no, you mustn't go out at night!" Eira said.

"Why?" Pru asked.

"Trolls! They've become more and more bold since . . . "—Eira glanced at her mother—"well, lately. They've been seen in the fields at night."

"You can sleep on the floor," Alva said. "There's plenty of room. You can be off on your way tomorrow."

"What do you think?" Pru asked ABE.

"It doesn't look like we have much choice. We're no match for trolls here." Their looking glasses could only banish Mythics from Earth, where they didn't belong. They'd be useless on Asgard.

"Okay," Pru said. "Thank you. Now, since you enjoyed the story so much, perhaps you'd like to pass the time by answering some questions about Baldur's death?"

"No," Alva said. "I would not. I must get these two to bed and get some sleep myself. Tomorrow will be a busy day. I have those four baskets of clothes to mend. That is how I earn *my* keep. Stories are fine, but they will not feed my family."

"That woman is so *stubborn*," Pru said to ABE when they stepped aside to discuss the situation.

"Yeah. But I've been thinking. Maybe we've been approaching this the wrong way. Have you noticed how she keeps mentioning how much work she has to do? Maybe if we could somehow help her with that, we could get her to talk to us."

"ABE, that's it! You're a genius!"

"I am?"

"Totally. And so am I. Because I have a brilliant plan."

"Ah, how brilliant exactly? And how much mortal danger does it involve?"

"Be quiet. Even you will like this one. Trust me."

CHAPTER 15

THE FIRE HAD FALLEN TO EMBERS AND SHADOWS FILLED THE SMALL HOME when Pru called out to Alva in a soft voice, so as not to wake up Sten or Eira.

"What is it, girl?" Alva said, also whispering.

"I have a secret to tell you. My friend and I haven't been completely honest with you."

"Oh?" Alva shuffled over to the corner of the room where Pru and ABE sat on blankets that had been placed over piles of hay.

"We are not who we told you. My friend here is Aloysius the Fierce. And I . . ." Pru passed for what ABE could only assume was dramatic effect, "I am Prudence the Red."

"Are you now?" Alva's tone suggested she did not properly appreciate dramatic effect.

"Yes. We're not just skalds. We're great heroes of Midgard, too, and friends of the gods. As such, we have access to great powers and magic."

"Is that so?"

"*Yes.* And because you've been so kind to us, we are going to give you a boom."

"*Boon,*" ABE corrected, assuming she meant a favor and not an explosion. Though with Pru you could never quite be sure.

"Right. *Boon.* When you wake up in the morning, you will find all your clothes mended. You will also find new clothes for you and your family to help you through the winter."

Wait. What? ABE tried to catch Pru's eye, but she ignored him.

"Of course, in return, it *would* be nice if you were to take some time and tell us about the events on the day Baldur died."

Alva stared at her while ABE held his breath. Finally, the woman snorted. It might have been a sound of amusement or disgust. "Child, you may the boldest liar I have ever met."

"I prefer Fibber," Pru said. "But I'm telling you the truth about this."

"Very well. You have a bargain. In return for your . . .

boon . . . I will answer any questions you have about the day the Fair One died. *But* I will do so in the morning. After you have delivered on your promise."

"Deal."

Alva snorted again, then walked off to her rest.

"Pru," ABE whispered, "what are you doing? Where are we supposed to come up with all those clothes? And where's Ratatosk gone?"

"Don't worry," Pru said. "It's all part of the plan."

"Thor's hammer!"

ABE sat up, instantly awake. He brushed hay from his hair and squinted in the bright glow of morning. "What is it? Where are we?"

Alva stood in the center of the room. Her hands were clasped to her cheeks. In front of her, where there had been four baskets the night before, sat no fewer than *ten* baskets. Neatly folded clothing filled every one. Eira and Sten knelt among the baskets and explored their contents with excitement.

"Mother, look at the weave on this dress! It's the finest I've ever seen!" Eira said, holding up a garment.

"*How?*" Alva said, turning to Pru. "How did you do this?"

"Sorry," Pru said, sitting on her pile of hay. "Explanations weren't part of the deal."

Alva said nothing for a moment. Her eyes went

from Pru to the baskets. ABE crossed his fingers and watched to see how the woman would react.

"No. No, they were not. Very well. A bargain is a bargain, girl. Sten and Eira, go outside until I call for you. I have things to discuss with our guests."

Alva's two children said their good-byes, and Alva seated herself on a chair near the hearth.

"Go on, then, children. Ask your questions."

Pru blinked. She seemed too surprised that her plan had worked to think of a question.

"Were you there when Loki . . . when Baldur was killed?" ABE asked, jumping in.

"I was. I was cleaning blankets in a corner of the yard where the gods had gathered."

"So you saw what happened?" Pru asked, recovering.

"I did." Alva lifted her chin. There was a quivering about her lips that seemed out of place on her strong, confident face.

"I'm sorry," ABE said. "I am. It must have been awful. But . . . we have to ask. Can you tell us what you saw?"

"Why, boy?" Alva snapped. "Why must you make me relive it? You *know* the story. We all do. The Allfather told it long before it happened."

"Yes, but now that it *has* happened, we need the details," Pru said. "So . . . so we can tell the story better."

"The old story has been around so long," ABE said. "And stories change."

"So be it." Alva took a deep breath and began. "It was a feast day. A celebration. The gods gathered at Breidablik as they often did. Baldur was the fairest and most beloved of all, and his home the most beautiful. The celebration became boisterous. And, as was so often the case, the gods fell to their favorite sport, throwing weapons at Baldur."

"Some sport," Pru muttered.

ABE shushed her. He didn't want to interrupt Alva. The gods' choice of games did seem odd. But he had expected it from the myth of Baldur's death. The story described how Odin had used his power as Allfather to magically protect his beloved son from almost everything on the three worlds. Only mistletoe had escaped Odin's notice, but it was considered too small a plant to cause any harm. Baldur's near invulnerability had given rise to the peculiar sport Alva had witnessed.

"As had always happened before, the weapons they threw bounced off Baldur. No blade or bow could pierce the charms of protection Odin had placed on his son. Until . . ."

Alva hung her head. ABE waited silently for her to continue, as did Pru.

"Until the spear struck him and pierced his chest.

Wooden, and worked through with oil from the mistletoe plant it was. Everything stopped when that spear struck. There was no movement. No sound. Even Baldur did not cry out. He just stood there, run through by the spear, the dew of slaughter spilling from the wound in his chest."

Alva dabbed her eyes with her apron before continuing.

"The first sound came from Thor. No thunder, no rage. The cry that came from his throat was too powerful to be contained by any storm. He ran to the Shining One's side and caught him as he fell. Thor wept as his brother died in his arms. They all wept, all the gods, all the goddesses, all of us. Everything and everyone wept as Baldur's light died. All but one."

"Loki?" ABE guessed.

"Father of wolves and worms! Trickster to the gods! Bringer of death! He had no tears to shed for the fairest of the gods."

"He was there?" Pru asked. "Loki? You're sure?"

"Of course I'm sure. I know the liar's face. It haunts my dreams!"

"Did you see Loki throw the spear?" ABE asked.

"No. Blind Hod threw the spear. Poor fool. He threw what had been given to him. He meant no harm. He only wanted to be part of the game."

"So it was whoever gave Hod the spear laced with mistletoe that wanted Baldur dead," ABE said.

"Did you see who gave Hod the spear?" Pru pressed. "Was it Loki?"

Alva frowned. "I did not see. I was distracted by my work. I did not look up until after the deed was done. But I *did* see the trickster slither away after the fact, snake that he is!"

"You're *sure*?" Pru asked. "You're sure you saw Loki slipping away?"

"I'm sure," Alva said. "He went right past me as he fled."

ABE broke the silence that filled the room after Alva's pronouncement. "Thank you, Alva. I'm sorry you had to relive all that. I guess we should go."

"One last thing," Pru burst out. "I have to ask. Why did the gods do it? Why did they make sport out of throwing weapons at Baldur? They *knew* what would happen. Couldn't anyone have stopped Hod from throwing the spear?"

"Can you stop the will of the Fates, child?" Alva said, sounding shocked. "Are the gods such cowards that they would try? No! Each played their role, as they were and are fated to do."

As her initial wave of outrage passed, Alva's voice took on a softer tone.

"Besides, no one expected the fateful throw to come that day. Hod had thrown a thousand spears over the years. No one attended to that throw. It was such a shock. Even knowing it would happen one day. No one thought it would be *that* day. I suppose no one ever thinks it is their day. We all hope for more time. The end should always come tomorrow, never today."

*

"How *did* you do it?" ABE asked Pru as they left the village behind. "How did you get all those clothes?"

"Simple! Last night, I sent Ratatosk back to the Henhouse with a message for Mister Fox. Ratatosk told him that I needed the clothes, and why."

"Of course!" ABE said. "So Mister Fox had the *domovye* mend and make the clothes."

"Right. And apparently it worked. The clothes were there before I woke up this morning. The *domovye* must have slipped in and out while everyone was asleep. They're good at that, too."

"Pru . . . that plan was *brilliant*!"

"I told you so," Pru said. She grinned and added, "But thanks."

They reached the Henhouse in short order and found Mister Fox waiting in the same sitting room they'd encountered on their last visit. He paced the small room, stopping only when they both entered.

"It's about time," he said.

"Well, excuse us for being late," Pru answered. "We were busy out there getting the job done."

"You're right. I'm sorry." Mister Fox pinched the

bridge of his nose. "And I'm eager to hear what you've learned. Sit. Tell me what happened."

ABE and Pru each took a chair. Mister Fox remained standing, leaning on the back of his seat. His foot tapped lightly on the floor.

"Well, it took some work," Pru began, "but I think we found out everything we could."

She recited the events of the morning and previous day. ABE supplied details as needed. Otherwise, he let Pru have her moment. After all, it had been her clever idea that had earned them the information they'd been looking for.

Mister Fox scratched his nose while he processed everything he'd heard. When they finished, he said, "Well done, you two. The trick with the clothing was inspired. So what do we know?"

"We know now that Loki *was* there when Baldur died," ABE said.

"And he ran off when Baldur got killed. Not a good sign," Pru added.

"No," Mister Fox agreed. "It's not. But it's not proof, either. Your witness, Alva, didn't see him give the spear to Hod."

The detective pressed a hand to his temples, massaging them with his thumb and index finger for a moment before pulling the hand down his long face. He looked . . . worried. ABE couldn't remember Mister

Fox ever looking worried before. He felt a pang of sympathy for the detective and lingering guilt for doubting him earlier.

"Like you said, though, we don't have proof. I mean, we don't know for sure that Loki gave Hod the spear to throw."

"Wait," Pru said, swiveling in her seat to look at him. "Now you're defending Loki? Do you really think he's innocent?"

ABE ran a hand through his hair. "No. Not really."

"I appreciate the thought, though, ABE," Mister Fox said. "Bottom line? You two accomplished a lot, but our investigation isn't done. We'll discuss next steps when you come back tomorrow."

"You're sending us home?" ABE asked.

"But we're in the zone!" Pru said. "And you said you'd tell us your theory about ABE's dream when we got back."

"Things have changed. I didn't expect you to spend the night. I don't want to keep you in Agsard any longer than I have to."

"What's the big deal?" Pru asked. "You can still get us back to the moment after we left, right?"

"Yes. But that's not the point."

"So what *is* the point?"

"Well, in part, Ratatosk had to go tend to some of his own business for a bit. Delivering messages. Or gathering acorns. I don't know. Whatever mischievous squirrels do for their day job. I'd like him to be here when we pick things up again. We're going to need him."

"You could still tell us what you think about who sent my dream," ABE said.

"I could, yes. I *could*. But I'm not going to."

"How come?" Pru demanded.

"Because it won't change anything if you wait a day, and I think it will drive you both a little crazy to *have* to wait. It's petty, I know, but I think a little retaliation is in order."

"Retaliation? For what?" Pru said as the Henhouse launched itself into the air.

"*Surprisingly little. Mostly, he got in the way and made sarcastic remarks*," Mister Fox quoted, repeating Pru's words about him from the night before.

Pru sank into her chair with a groan as ABE remembered Mister Fox's attempt to contact them through the looking glass. He must have heard Pru's story before closing the connection. ABE considered pointing out that Pru had told the story, not him, but it occurred to him that he hadn't spoken in the detective's defense.

"So, uh, I guess we'll just get going then," Pru said as the henhouse landed.

Mister Fox smiled sweetly and waved good-bye.

CHAPTER 16

ABE AND PRU PARTED WAYS WHEN THEY RETURNED TO MIDDLETON. IT WAS weird to think that even though they'd spent the night in Asgard, it was still the same afternoon they'd left Earth. ABE saw kids with their backpacks on, heading home from the first day of school.

He was just a couple of doors down from his house—he could see his dad stretching on the front steps for a run—when he heard the sound of kids on bikes behind him. He stepped onto his neighbor's lawn to make room for them to pass.

As they rode by, ABE recognized the riders as Danny and another boy from his homeroom whose name he didn't know.

"Hey, look," Danny called, turning his bike onto

the empty street to make a slow loop beside ABE. "It's forsooth boy. I wish you good day, forsooth boy!"

ABE hung his head as Danny completed his loop and rode off, laughing with his friend.

Walking up to his house, he greeted his dad without meeting his eyes and went inside. He hoped that would be the end of it—but he knew it wouldn't be. His dad followed him into the kitchen.

"ABE, what just happened?"

"It's nothing, Dad," ABE said as he opened the fridge. He'd been starving during the walk home. Now he'd lost his appetite. "It's just a kid from school being a jerk."

"Yeah, I can see he's a jerk. I couldn't miss it. But I'm not talking about him. I'm talking about you. ABE, you can't just let that kind of thing happen. You *have* to learn how to stick up for yourself. Even if it means getting knocked down a time or two. Otherwise, people are going to walk all over you for the rest of your life."

"I know, Dad. I just . . . I've got a lot on my mind right now. Is it okay if I grab a snack and head up to my room?"

His dad looked like he was about to say something more but shrugged. "Okay. If that's what you have to do."

ABE watched him go. Then he closed the fridge

and climbed the stairs to his room, empty-handed. Danny's laughter echoed in his head.

So did something else, though.

Forsooth.

Something about the word nagged at him.

But he wasn't in the mood for riddles at the moment. Reaching his room, he knelt by his bookshelf and looked for another world to escape into.

The next day at school, ABE sat with the other kids in his homeroom in a circle on the carpet in the front of the room. So far as he knew, their class was the only one that had what Mr. Jeffries called a Morning Meeting.

Each meeting began with everyone in the circle greeting someone else. After that, three kids could share something that was on their minds or going on in their lives. Then, if there was time, they would play a quick game before heading off to their first class.

Most teachers wouldn't have been able to pull off something like that. A few kids made jokes about how ridiculous they thought Morning Meetings were. Danny was the most outspoken—though of course he only said something when he was sure Mr. Jeffries wouldn't hear.

But most of the conversations ABE overheard suggested that the other kids really liked Mr. Jeffries so far.

ABE did. He was pretty sure Pru did, too, even though she wouldn't admit it. So most of them were willing to give him the benefit of the doubt when it came to Morning Meetings.

That morning they finished up early, and Mr. Jeffries asked if everyone knew how to play Telephone.

Most of the kids did. Mr. Jeffries would whisper a sentence into the ear of the person sitting next to him. That person would whisper the same sentence, as she or he had heard it, into the ear of the next person, and so on. The idea was that, by the end, the sentence would usually break down into an absurd series of words because one person would mishear something—and that misunderstanding would get passed on and added to.

It reminded ABE of how myths changed over time.

Sure enough, by the time the girl next to him, Isabella, whispered the sentence to ABE it was: "Blue chickens eat pimply avocados." Isabella could barely say it with a straight face and shrugged to suggest she'd done her best.

ABE whispered the message to Pru, who passed it on to Danny, who sat at about the midpoint of the circle.

As soon as she finished, Danny leaned away and threw up his hands.

"Whoa, Mr. Jeffries. I don't know what you said, but

I'm pretty sure you wouldn't want me to repeat what Pru just said to me. That was totally inappropriate."

"What? I didn't say anything bad!" Pru insisted, turning red in the face. That started a domino effect, with everyone in the circle quickly denying that *they* had been the one to say anything wrong. The room quickly exploded into chaos.

"STOP!"

It was the first time Mr. Jeffries had raised his voice. Everyone immediately quieted.

"I'm disappointed," he said. His voice returned to a regular volume but his face was slightly red. "We don't have to do this. We could have a homeroom where everyone sits silently until the day starts. I happen to think that school can and should be fun, though. And I think that one of the best ways to build a community is to play games together. But that doesn't work if you all can't handle it."

Most kids in the class wore sheepish expressions and avoided looking Mr. Jeffries in the eye. ABE glanced at Danny. His head was ducked and he was hiding a smile.

"Tomorrow, we're going to try a different game. I hope it goes better. I would hate for us to have to stop because of the actions of one person, whoever that one person was." Mr. Jeffries's eyes settled on Pru.

"It wasn't me!" she said.

"I didn't say it was."

"So why are you looking at me like that, then?" Pru stood up.

ABE winced at the hurt in Pru's voice.

"I have to go to the restroom," she said. She stormed out of the room without waiting for Mr. Jeffries's response.

Mr. Jeffries watched her go, his mouth set in a firm line. Turning back to the class, he said, "Everyone can take a book out until the bell rings."

ABE reached into his backpack. For once, though, he didn't feel like reading. He wanted to go check on Pru, but he had a feeling that Mr. Jeffries wouldn't let anyone else leave the room at that point.

ABE let his eyes wander. By chance, they happened to land on the poster with the poem that Mr. Jeffries had read on the night of the open house:

Children, ay, forsooth . . .

Danny's mockery from the day before came back to him. The sting of it had lessened overnight. ABE considered why the word had caught his attention. *Forsooth.*

Of course!

He straightened in his seat. At least something good had come of the day.

ABE had just figured out the riddle from his dream. And it wasn't about Mister Fox at all!

CHAPTER 17

PRU HADN'T RETURNED TO HOMEROOM BEFORE THE BELL RANG, SO ABE caught up with her at lunch, eager to share his discovery. She had other things on her mind, though.

"I have to stay after school today to talk to Mr. Jeffries."

"Oh. Sorry. That wasn't fair at all."

"Tell me about it." Pru shoved the food around on her cafeteria tray.

"I'll wait for you."

"No, you go on to the Henhouse. I'll meet you there. I have a feeling I'm going to need some space after Mr. Jeffries and I *talk*."

✶

The Henhouse's ribbed hallway opened to the vast inner courtyard ABE had grown used to during his first visits to the magical structure. A *domovoi* met him there and gestured with floating hands for him to follow.

ABE expected the *domovoi* to take him to the oculus room. Instead, they entered an unfamiliar section of the Henhouse. The *domovoi* paused in front of a set of arched double doors at the end of a long hallway. ABE breathed in the familiar heavy scent of the forest, but it seemed stronger there. Opening the doors and stepping through, he instantly understood why.

The room beyond the double doors was, without question, the most wonderful place ABE had ever seen.

It was a library.

It was a forest.

It was *both.*

At first, the interior of the room looked normal enough. In fact, it looked a lot like the Henhouse's inner courtyard. Columns rose up on either side of the door, carved like trees. The pattern of columns repeated itself for about ten feet in every direction.

Then, gradually, they changed. The columns began to look more realistic. After about twenty feet they no longer *looked* like trees, they *were* trees. Actual trees! Massive branches, heavy with leaves, stretched out above him as ABE walked along. The branches hid the ceiling and offered refuge to the many birds that flew overhead. ABE even glimpsed something that flew like a bird but seemed reptilian and had bat wings. Could it have been a tiny dragon?

Lost in his study of the treetops, ABE tripped. Looking down, he saw that the polished planks of the floorboards had all but vanished beneath a mossy scrub. The walls of the library had also given way to the forest and disappeared. He could only make out the door, in the distance, through which he'd entered, lightly lit by the oil lamps that hung on either side.

ABE clambered up an embankment, turning his head in every direction to take in the splendor around him. As astonishing as the living forest was, the books were what made the space truly spectacular.

There were books *everywhere.* They sat on bookshelves that seemed to grow out of the landscape. Some shelves stretched between trees while others appeared to have been carved into boulders. ABE even found a collection of Arthurian legends stacked within a hollowed-out tree trunk.

Crossing a quaint wooden bridge over a creek, ABE discovered an area ahead that appeared to be an oasis of ordered architecture among the wilds of the living library. Tables stood together on a surface that was more floor than ground, in front of a fireplace whose chimney disappeared into the thick branches overhead.

To the left of the fireplacc, a two-story section of wall stood independent of any other structure. A walkway, supported by tree branches that gradually morphed into support timbers, separated the two stories.

Mister Fox stood on the walkway, examining the shelves. He removed a book and turned as ABE approached. "Just you today?"

"What? No, Pru's coming. Mister Fox—what *is* this place?"

"It's the library, of course. I thought you of all people would recognize that."

"No, I see that. It's just . . . wow. So many books." ABE shook his head and tried to focus his thoughts. *So many books!* "But how come it's like this?"

The detective climbed down a ladder from the walkway and joined him. He placed the leather-bound book he'd selected on a nearby table.

"It's like this *because* it's the library," Mister Fox explained. "Magic is all about possibility. What is magic, after all, if not the possibility of something *more*, something fantastic, beyond our everyday experience? Well, books are possibility made real. Think about it. Every page turn, every new chapter represents the possibility of something new. A single book is magic. Now, imagine a room full of books, or a building. Libraries are focal points for wild magic. Not just here. Everywhere."

"Wait. Really?"

"Of course. Think back to libraries you've visited. You've felt it. Walking down the aisles among the shelves—a prickling of energy. A tingling just on the edge of your senses, teasing you. Just out of reach. Why do you think libraries are such ordered places? Alphabetization. Dewey decimal system. Card catalogs. Enforced whispering."

"Card catalogs? Mister Fox, when's the last time you were actually *in* a library?"

"Doesn't matter. The point still stands. All those things, all those orderly systems, they've evolved over time to keep the wild magic in check. And it works out there in the world. But here? In the Henhouse? Oh, no. That's different. Here the wild library magic changes things. It takes the Henhouse's essence and makes it . . . *more* somehow."

"More what?"

"More Henhousey. You know what I mean. Columns that look like trees *become* trees. The *domovye* tend it. They keep it from spreading too much."

"It's beautiful."

Mister Fox closed his eyes and inhaled deeply. "Oh yes. It is, isn't it?"

The detective took one more breath. Then he opened his eyes. "So while we wait for your partner in crime, shall I tell you my theory about your dream?

It will drive Pru crazy if we both know something she doesn't."

"Actually, I think we should wait for Pru. She's had kind of a rough day. Anyway, there's something else I'd like to talk to you about."

"Be my guest." Mister Fox gestured to the table where he'd placed the book and invited ABE to join him there. "What's on your mind?"

"I've been thinking about Pru and me and our time yesterday in Asgard. And I've been thinking about how eager you were to get us home once we returned to the Henhouse."

"Oh?"

"Yeah. See, I was thinking about when Loki and Gristling kidnapped me last year. I was so scared. I still have nightmares, actually. But looking back, I don't really remember feeling very homesick. A little. I wanted to get away. And I wanted to go home. But I only remember wanting to go home because it was somewhere safe. I don't remember thinking a lot about my mom or dad after a while. And the thing is . . . I kind of felt the same way this time. I hardly thought of home at all while we were gone."

ABE paused, hoping Mister Fox would say something. He pushed on when the detective remained quiet.

"You said we slip from the minds of people on Earth

when we travel to Worlds of Myth. So I was wondering . . . does it work both ways? Do people on Earth slip from *our* minds when we go traveling?"

"You're a very clever young man," Mister Fox said with a tip of his hat. "Yes, ABE. That's exactly what happens."

"So if we spent enough time on a World of Myth . . ."

"You could forget your homes, forget your families. And you could be forgotten in turn. And the potential danger is greater than you realize. The effect is cumulative. The more often you travel to a World of Myth, the harder it can be to reconnect with the people you left behind. And the more time you spend there, the quicker you forget."

"Why didn't you tell us?"

"Because you're nowhere close to the threshold of danger. You could spend weeks, maybe months, traveling back and forth before suffering any ill effects. But I'm always conservative about how much time I keep Fibbers away from their homes. You just never know what could happen."

ABE paused to let that sink in. He still couldn't help feeling like the detective should have told them. But that wasn't the only thing that bothered him, or even the thing that bothered him most.

"Mister Fox . . . would we have seen you again if the Mythics hadn't come back to Middleton?"

The detective stared into the flames blazing in the nearby fireplace for a long time before answering.

"No, ABE. Probably not. Earth and Worlds of Myth have grown too far apart. You can't live in both. Not for long, anyway. Not anymore. If you or Pru or any of the children who have worked with me as Fibbers over the years were to spend too much time in the Henhouse or in Worlds of Myth, then eventually you'd grow estranged from your home and your families. It's better if, when I go, I stay gone."

Mister Fox paused, and ABE realized he wasn't staring into the fire anymore. He was gazing at a painting hanging over the fireplace mantle. It showed an elderly woman dressed in traditional Russian garb, with a babushka tied under her chin. She had a wise face and a kind smile.

"That's Baba Yaga, isn't it?" ABE asked softly.

"Yes. It's how she looked when I last saw her."

"Is she still alive?" ABE blushed. "Sorry. I just . . . I remember the story you told us last year of how you met . . . I couldn't tell . . ."

"It's okay, ABE. The truth is that I don't know if she's still alive. If she is, she's somewhere in the thrice-tenth kingdom, the Russian World of Myth. It's a beautiful place, with soaring palaces, flocks of magical birds, and wish-granting fish. But there's no way for me to know if Baba Yaga is still there. It's someplace I can't go anymore."

Mister Fox fell silent. ABE wasn't sure what to say.

Well, he was sure. It just wasn't going to be easy.

"You have to tell Pru. You have to tell her she won't see you again once you're done here."

"Do I?" Mister Fox's question sounded sincere. "Is that kinder, do you think?"

When ABE didn't answer immediately, Mister Fox leaned back in his chair.

"You're a good friend, ABE. Pru is lucky to have you. It took courage for you to come here and confront me about this."

"Courage? Me?"

"You sound surprised."

"Well, yeah. I mean, that's not really my thing. Pru's the brave one. I'm the one that's always scared."

"Is that what you think? Do you really think that's what your story is about, ABE? Finding courage?"

"I don't know. Maybe. My dad doesn't think I stand up for myself enough."

"Ah. What do you think?"

"I guess he's right."

"And you think that's because you're scared?" Mister Fox tapped his chin with his long index finger. "No. No, I don't see it."

"You don't?"

"No. Ever since I met you, ABE, I've seen you stand up for and stand by your friends, no matter what. Whether it means going back to face the giants who kidnapped you or confronting an eccentric detective about emotionally abandoning your best friend, I have never seen you back down from doing what's right for the people you care about. Not once. If you think that isn't *courage*, then you don't know the meaning of the word. And between you and me, Aloysius, the likelihood of you not knowing the meaning of the word is very small indeed."

"Maybe," ABE said, shrugging.

"You don't sound convinced."

"I don't know. I'd like to be courageous. I feel like I'm supposed to be. You say I'm brave. My parents gave me a name that means 'famous warrior.' Thor thinks I should embrace my fierce nature. Even the lady from my dream called me 'young hero.' But none of those things feel like me."

"Good."

"Good?"

"Yes. Good. Don't get me wrong. I'm sorry that struggling with other people's expectations of you is causing you pain. But it's good you're struggling. Consider the other option. You could surrender to others' expectations. But I think that would just cause you more pain in the long run."

Mister Fox leaned forward and folded his hands on the table.

"ABE, there are always going to be people in life who want to tell you who you're supposed to be. Parents. Teachers. Friends. Enemies. It doesn't matter how old you get. There are always going to be roles you're expected to play. The important thing to remember is that it's *your* life. You'll get to the *you* that you're meant to be. I know the possibilities seem overwhelming, like—well, like books in a library. But you'll get there. Until then, remember that there's nothing worse than having to play a role that someone else gives you. There's nothing worse than letting someone else define who you are. That way lies misery."

ABE didn't know what to say. He couldn't remember anyone talking to him in such an honest way ever before. Before ABE could think of a response, Pru stormed into view.

"Mister Fox! We need to take the Henhouse somewhere—*fast*!"

CHAPTER 18

MISTER FOX ROSE FROM HIS CHAIR, INSTANTLY ALERT.

"What is it?" ABE asked. "What's happened? Where do we need to go?"

"We need to take the Henhouse to school and drop it on our teacher, Mr. Jeffries."

The detective sat back down.

"I can't do that, Pru," he said.

"Why? You dropped it on Gristling last year. Now when I need a *tiny* favor, you're suddenly all moral about dropping your house on people?"

"A little bit, yes. But just to save some time, let me be clearer. I literally *can't* do that. I told you last year that the Henhouse is very limited in where it can set foot." The detective turned to ABE. "And no, ABE, I'm not making a pun on the word *foot.*"

ABE closed his mouth, disappointed.

"The point," Mister Fox continued, "is that when it's on Earth, the Henhouse can only land in places where Earth and Worlds of Myth intersect, what I call the Borderlands. That's true of all witch's houses. The Henhouse, however, has the added limitation that it can only set down on grounds that border the living and the dead. Graveyards, cemeteries, and the like."

"Right. You think it's because you're mortal and not a witch," ABE said, remembering.

"Precisely. Which is why we can't use the Henhouse to squash your teacher, Pru. Sorry."

"Fine. Then I want a hammer. Thor has a hammer. *I* want a hammer," Pru said, throwing herself into a chair next to ABE's. She glanced around and added, grudgingly, "Nice library, by the way. What happened to the old one?"

"The room you saw last year? That was just a workshop, a space I use for a specific project. I set that one up during our last investigation specifically to study the Middleton Stone. And while we're on the subject of Thor's hammer and things related to Norse mythology, perhaps we can return to our navigation?"

While Mister Fox collected the leather-bound book

he'd taken from the shelves earlier and paged through it, ABE whispered to Pru, "Things didn't go well with Mr. Jeffries?"

"I don't want to talk about it."

ABE leaned back, frowning.

"Okay," Mister Fox said, turning the book to show ABE and Pru the page he'd been seeking. "ABE, have you ever seen this woman before?"

ABE gasped.

"That's the woman from my dream!" The book was a handwritten journal and the image was a pencil drawing, but it was unquestionably of the woman from his dream. The likeness was uncanny, even if half of the woman's face was so heavily shaded that it looked like a black shadow.

"Not a dream, ABE," Mister Fox corrected. "A nightmare."

"Well, yeah. Technically, I guess."

"The distinction is actually important in this case. Do either of you know what a mare is?"

"It's a horse!" Pru blurted. "Sorry, ABE. Beat you to that one. Not that I have a thing about horses!"

ABE decided that was the perfect time to not bring up her unicorn pajamas.

"Well, yes," Mister Fox said. "But in this case, that's not the answer I was looking for. A mare is also the name for a creature from Norse mythology. It's a spirit that visits people when they're sleeping. They deliver bad dreams and, sometimes, messages. The two meanings are connected, actually. The spirit is said to sit on the sleeper's chest, riding him, in a sense."

"So you're saying one of those things—those mares—was in my room with me?" ABE shivered, remembering the flurry of movement by his window.

"But who sent it?" Pru asked. "And who's the woman in the dream—the woman in that book?"

"Well, that's where things get interesting. The woman in ABE's dream is Hel, though she prefers to go by her title as ruler of Niflheim—the Queen of the Dead."

"Whoa," Pru said.

"And I'm guessing she's the one who sent the mare in the first place. Mares are creatures of Niflheim. They go where the queen sends them."

"So the queen sent the mare to carry a message to ABE," Pru said. "But in his dream, the woman said the message came from someone else. Who gave her the message in the first place?"

"I think I might know," ABE said.

"Who, ABE?" Mister Fox asked.

"I think maybe Loki sent the message."

"What?" Pru exclaimed.

"Why do you think that?" Mister Fox pressed, his nose twitching.

"Well, I was thinking about the riddle today. Our teacher, Mr. Jeffries, has a quote on his wall. One of the words in it is *forsooth.*"

"So?" Pru asked.

"It got me thinking. Remember what *sooth* means? It's another word for *truth.* The riddle talks about a truth-teller. But if we turn that phrase around a little bit, it becomes *sooth-teller* . . . or *soothsayer.* A sooth-sayer is someone who can see the future. Like Odin."

ABE took a deep breath, and forced himself to slow down. He always got excited when explaining riddles.

"Remember what Mister Fox said about the riddle's meaning? He said someone could not be telling the truth if they didn't know what the truth was. So what if the riddle really means Odin's wrong? *When is a truth-teller not telling the truth?*"

"When he's wrong," Pru said. "So the Queen of the Dead sent ABE a message from Loki saying that Odin's vision is wrong? But why send the message to ABE?"

"That makes sense, if you think about it," ABE said. "Loki knows I like riddles and word games. That's how I figured out he was disguised as Fay Loningtime last year. He saw me change the letters around to spell 'I am often lying.'"

"But why use a riddle? Why not just say he's innocent?" Pru asked.

"I've been wondering that myself," Mister Fox said, at last chiming in. "It's the one bit I haven't been able to figure out."

"So you think we're right," Pru said.

"I do. I figured out that the phrase *truth-teller* was a reference to Odin, a soothsayer, almost immediately."

"Why didn't you say anything?" ABE asked. "You let me think the riddle was about you!"

"Because I didn't trust my judgment." Mister Fox rose and walked to the fire. "You were right yesterday, ABE. I do want Loki to be innocent. But I only told you both part of the reason why. It's true that I want to avoid Ragnarok. But I also want Odin to be *wrong.*"

"Why?" Pru asked, taking the word out of ABE's mouth. "Why is it so important to you that Odin is wrong."

The detective turned to face them.

"Because if Loki *is* guilty, if Odin's visions are right, then I'm as good as—"

"As good as what?" Pru asked when he didn't finish.

"As good as useless," Mister Fox said, pinching the bridge of his nose. "Don't you see? What am I always telling you two? 'Don't believe it. Don't be so sure.' Odin was right. Uncertainty *is* my religion. But if Odin's visions are always accurate, then the future is set. There *is* no uncertainty. It doesn't exist! I don't know how I fit into that world. I'm not sure I do."

ABE and Pru looked at each other. Neither knew what to say. Finally, ABE took a deep breath.

"Okay," he said. "But this is good news, isn't it? If we're right about the riddle, then Loki is trying to tell us he's innocent. That would mean that Mister Fox is right and Odin is wrong."

"But how do we know Loki is telling the truth?" Pru asked. "Just because he says he's innocent doesn't mean it's true."

"I'm afraid Pru's right," Mister Fox said. "We need proof."

"But we've run out of witnesses," ABE said. "The gods didn't see anything. Alva didn't see anything. There's no one left who can tell us who gave Hod the spear that killed Baldur."

"That's not entirely true," Mister Fox said, returning to the table.

"It's not?" Pru asked. "Who else is left?"

"Isn't it obvious? We have to talk to Baldur."

"Baldur?" Pru and ABE said at the exact same time.

"But he's dead!" ABE added.

"Exactly," Mister Fox said. "Which means we know just where to find him."

"You mean . . . you want us to go to Niflheim?" Pru asked. "You want us to go to the world of the dead?"

"That's a terrible idea! *The world of the dead*?" ABE tried to come up with a way to explain to Mister Fox just how bad an idea it was. "But that's, like, a world . . . full of dead people!"

"Very articulate, ABE, but—"

"How will we avoid the zombies?" Pru asked. She sounded both frightened and curious.

"Zombies? What? No. Wait, you two. Listen. Niflheim is the world of the dead, yes. But there aren't zombies or walking skeletons there. Many mythologies include an underworld. There's a reason for that. Mythics are magical beings. When their corporeal forms die, their magical essence abides for a time in their version of the underworld. The people in Niflheim will look like people . . . for the most part."

"No zombies?" Pru asked.

"None."

"I still think this is a terrible idea," ABE said, pressing his forehead to the table.

"Don't worry," he heard Pru say to Mister Fox. "He says that a lot."

"You should be happy, ABE," Mister Fox said.

ABE looked up. "I should? Why?"

"Because you're about to go meet the girl of your dreams."

*

ABE waited for Pru and Mister Fox on the other end of the library's bridge. The detective had asked for a moment alone with Pru before she and ABE left for

Niflheim. ABE assumed he wanted to tell Pru that he would be leaving for good once their investigation was over.

Sure enough, Pru's eyes were red when she crossed the bridge a short time later. Mister Fox wasn't with her.

"Are you okay?" ABE asked.

"Yeah," Pru said.

"Really? I thought you'd be more upset."

"I guess I'm not really surprised."

"You're not?"

"No. I didn't really expect him to be in Niflheim."

"Wow. You're taking this better than I thought you would. Wait . . . what? You didn't expect who to be in Niflheim?"

"My dad."

"What?"

"That's what Mister Fox wanted to talk to me about. He wanted to make sure I understood that Niflheim was only a place where Mythics from Norse mythology went, not people from Earth. He didn't want me to be disappointed when my dad wasn't there."

"Oh!" ABE said, surprised. "That's ridiculous, though! Of course your dad wouldn't be there."

"Thanks, ABE," Pru said, charging past him and shoving his shoulder as she went. "You don't have to rub it in that I was being silly."

"No! Pru, wait! That's not what I meant at all. It's just . . . according to the myths, heroes don't go to Niflheim when they die. Your dad would never have been there. He was a hero."

Pru stopped and turned. He had thought that Pru couldn't surprise him anymore, but the hug she gave him then—fierce and honest—surprised him more than almost anything in his life.

"So, um, where's Mister Fox?" ABE asked, rubbing the back of his neck as Pru stepped away.

"He's going to meet us in the entryway. First, the *domovye* will take us somewhere to change into special clothes for Niflheim. I guess it's pretty cold there. So are you ready for the world of the dead?"

"Absolutely not. But let's get going, anyway."

ABE, PRU, AND MISTER FOX GATHERED IN THE ENTRYWAY OF THE HENHOUSE. ABE tugged at the collar of the shirt Mister Fox had given him. It was similar to the one he'd worn for the trip to Asgard but much thicker, as were his new pants. He also had a *domovoi*-crafted coat, hat, and gloves to protect him against Niflheim's cold.

"There are rules in Niflheim," Mister Fox was saying. "Some of them were made by the queen, some of them bind her. She has no dominion over living things, for example. That includes both of you. But two things can change that, so *don't* do either of those two things."

"What two things?" Pru asked.

"You can't take anything while you're in Niflheim.

Take no souvenirs, accept no gifts. Do not put yourself in debt to her. The Queen of the Dead keeps what is hers. If you take something from the queen, you become part of her horde. *Forever.* So take nothing. Nothing precious, nothing prized. Understand?"

"Got it," Pru said.

"What's the other thing we should avoid?" ABE asked.

"Dying," Mister Fox said. "Definitely avoid dying."

"*Very* helpful," Pru said.

"I try." Mister Fox stepped forward and opened the door. "You should be fine. The queen sent ABE that message. That doesn't mean she sees you as friends. But at least it means she's not openly hostile to you. Still, don't take anything for granted. The queen is the Norse personification of death. She's impossible to predict and harder to understand. Be careful."

"We will!" ABE said.

"Good. For what it's worth, the journey should be straightforward. Ratatosk will lead you due south through the landscape of Niflheim, right to the City of the Dead at the base of the Mountains of Mist. Time and distance will blur, just like it did on Asgard. You'll be at the city before you know it."

"That's what I'm afraid of," ABE said.

"You won't find anything to worry about in the bulk of the city itself. It was built to house those who die during Ragnarok. You'll find it mostly empty at this point. The Palace of the Dead sits at the southernmost edge of the city. That's where the queen lives and that's where things will get tricky. Be on your guard and remember what I told you."

ABE followed Pru onto the steps of the Henhouse. She paused there and looked back at the detective.

"You're sure about the no zombies thing, right?"

"Absolutely," Mister Fox said.

"Good," she said.

"Just be sure to watch out for the dragon," Mister Fox added with a wink. Then he closed the door.

"*Dragon?*" ABE squeaked.

An odd snorting came from above. ABE thought it might even be that of a dragon, until Ratatosk dropped onto his shoulder and he recognized the squirrel's laughter.

"Nidhogg's nowhere near—no, no. Big Nose is joking."

"You're sure?" ABE asked, and Ratatosk nodded confidently.

"So which way?" Pru asked after greeting Ratatosk with an affectionate scratch on his nose.

Ratatosk chittered happily at the attention and then nodded in the direction they should go. He did not abandon his perch on ABE's shoulder. Apparently, he intended to hitch a ride.

As he looked around Niflheim, ABE's chest tightened in panic. For a minute, he was sure that he was back in his dream! Bars rose up from the mist, trapping him. Gristling would appear any second and—

"ABE? *ABE!*" Pru gripped his shoulder. "Are you okay? You're white as a ghost."

"I . . . yeah. I'm okay." ABE shook off the panic as understanding settled in. He wasn't in his nightmare version of Asgard. Yggdrasil, the World Tree, had roots in all three worlds of Norse mythology. The Henhouse had simply landed at Yggdrasil's roots in Niflheim. Those roots were what he had mistaken for bars.

"It's like a haunted-house version of Asgard," Pru said, looking around.

ABE nodded. He had always enjoyed hikes in the woods in winter, when the leaves had all fallen and the branches were empty. But even in the coldest, darkest heart of winter, life survived in the forests on Earth. It could be hard to see, but it was there. The promise of renewal and rebirth lay just beneath the surface.

Not in Niflheim. The world of the dead stretched before them, a bleak alien landscape of mist and ice. Almost nothing lived there other than Yggdrasil's roots, and even they looked sick. ABE huddled in his coat and thought of cozy fires, hot chocolate, and his mother's vegetable soup. He thought of all the warmth of home and was comforted by not just the memories but also his ability to remember.

They had not walked far through the haunted tangles of Yggdrasil's roots when Ratatosk dug his claws into ABE's shoulder and hissed at Pru and him to stop.

"Wait here," the squirrel said. "Be still, be silent. Constrained. Composed. Closemouthed!"

"What is it?" Pru asked, but Ratatosk shushed her and jumped from ABE's shoulder. All but his tail disappeared into the fog. It cut through the mist like a submarine's periscope moving through a sea of vapor.

Ratatosk made his way toward a huge mound in the distance. It was about the size of a barn. ABE squinted. On second thought, maybe it was the size of *two* barns.

"Hey, Pru?" ABE whispered. "Does it look to you like that mound up ahead is getting bigger?

Pru's eyes widened and she grabbed ABE, pulling him behind the nearest root as a deep, booming voice echoed through the forest.

"RATATOSK! I THOUGHT I SMELLED SOMETHING UNPLEASANTLY ALIVE."

"Hello, Nidhogg," Ratatosk answered.

"Nidhogg?" ABE squeaked. "Nidhogg, *the dragon*?"

Pru clasped a hand over ABE's mouth as Ratatosk continued.

"I have a message for you," the squirrel said, clearing his throat.

ABE wiggled a finger in his ear. Had he heard that right? He knew that Ratatosk carried messages back and forth between Nidhogg and the eagle at the top of Yggdrasil. But did he have to do it *then*?

"Let's see," Ratatosk continued. "Ah yes! Eagle wants you to know that you 'are a cow-footed snake whose breath smells like the dung pile of a drove of a thousand swine.' Hmm! Eagle went for a focus on smells this time, yes, that I think was a nice departure."

Nidhogg roared and a crashing sound of wood splintering filled the air.

"Whurf's hahning?" ABE asked through Pru's fingers.

"What?" Pru asked, lowering her hand.

"What's happening?"

Pru peered around the edge of the root. She pulled back quickly. "Nidhogg is having a tantrum. He's biting through the roots and smashing them with his tail."

"You can see him? Is he big? What does he look like?"

Pru peeked again. She swallowed.

"You don't want to know."

ABE scrunched his eyes shut.

"TELL THAT LOATHSOME, OVERGROWN CHICKEN THAT HE FLIES ON THE UPDRAFTS OF HIS OWN FLATULENCE!"

"Yes, yes. Will do. I'm sure he'll be delighted to hear it."

Nidhogg roared. The sound of cracking wood filled

the air again. It grew gradually quieter, as though the dragon was moving away. Soon afterward, Ratatosk returned.

"I thought you said Nidhogg was nowhere near us when we got out of the Henhouse!" Pru said.

"He wasn't. No, no, no. It took some work to find him."

"*You mean we came looking for him?*" ABE asked.

"Of course! I have a job to do, after all! I can't play with you shortwits *all* the time!"

ABE and Pru eventually broke free of Yggdrasil's roots and found themselves on a vast plain that looked like the set of an old science fiction film for which most of the budget had been spent on fog machines and dried ice. Mist pooled along the ground as far as the eye could see. A few trees, withered and bare, rose from the mist, as did some rocks. Nearby mountains stabbed at the sky like jagged teeth.

The City of the Dead lay at the base of one of those mountains. ABE and Pru never would have reached it without Ratatosk's help. Three times they came to great chasms hidden in the fog. Ratatosk led them unfailingly to bridges that crossed each abyss. ABE felt sure that without him, they would have lost their footing and tumbled over the edge of an unseen chasm and down to the frozen river below.

They met their first nondragon resident of Niflheim at the final bridge, just before the city. An old woman who leaned heavily on a staff halted them with an upraised hand.

"What have we here, hmm?" the bent and bedraggled woman said. Matted hair hung over her face, and it was sometimes hard to tell where it ended and the animal skin rags that covered her body began. "Messenger, you are off your path. And who have you brought with you? Mortals! Still alive? A feast for Nidhogg, then."

"We're not a feast for anyone," Pru said, shivering. "Who are you?"

"I am Modgud, guardian of the bridge. Who are you, child, and what is your purpose?"

Ratatosk leaned in and whispered something in Pru's ear.

"I'm Pru. My friend ABE and I are here to talk to Baldur."

That was direct. Had Ratatosk told Pru to be honest? He'd clearly had dealings with Modgud before.

"Oh? Have you come to seek his release from the misty realm? You have traveled far for naught, then. It has been decided. The Queen of the Dead will keep what she has."

"We just want to talk to him," Pru said.

Modgud studied them a moment then turned back

to Pru. "Be warned, child. This path is not meant for mortal feet. I can see things in the mist, shapes of things to come. If you go this way, you will not return."

"What's she talking about?" ABE asked Ratatosk.

Ratatosk peered at Modgud.

"You have no authority to keep them," the squirrel said.

"I will not bar your way, Messenger, or the way of these children. I just tell you what will be."

"Can she really see the future?" Pru asked.

"The seeress of Niflheim knows strange things," Ratatosk said. "Not good, not good."

"What should we do?" ABE asked.

"We don't have any choice," Pru said. "We need answers. We have to talk to Baldur."

Pru stepped past Modgud and onto the bridge. ABE followed. They were halfway across when Modgud called out, "Farewell, children of Midgard. Give Modgud's greetings to the Queen of the Dead. We will not meet again on this journey."

Her cackling echoed through the chasm below, following them across the bridge and all the way to the gates of the City of the Dead.

"Who are they trying to keep out?" ABE asked, looking up at the gates. They hung on walls that rose even higher than the walls around Asgard.

"Not out, no, no, no. *In*," Ratatosk replied. "Like Modgud said, *The Queen of the Dead keeps what is hers.*"

Ratatosk was right about the walls not being there to keep anyone out of the city. Neither of the guards that stood on either side of the city's gates challenged ABE and Pru as they passed through.

The City of the Dead resembled Asgard in some respects. The basic architecture was about the same. But the timber in Niflheim was rotted. So was the stone somehow. And while Asgard had sparkled with gems and precious stones, the City of the Dead sparkled with ice and snow. Perhaps the greatest difference, though, was the absence of people.

"It really is empty," Pru said.

"The halls of the City of the Dead will overflow when Ragnarok comes," Ratatosk said. "Mostly empty now. Desolate. Untenanted."

Sure enough, they continued all the way to the palace without passing another soul.

Most of the city's buildings had been constructed from wood. The palace, however, was made from stone. It reminded ABE a little of Winterhaven House. The massive hall seemed to grow out of the mountain itself, just as solid—and somehow far more imposing. Bracing himself, he crossed the threshold and prepared to come face-to-face with the specter from his dream, the Queen of the Dead.

CHAPTER 20

THE QUEEN OF THE DEAD SAT IN THE HALL OF HER PALACE. SHE WAS beautiful.

And she was terrible.

Her left side was lovely. The queen's black hair and ripe, red lips were just as beautiful as ABE remembered them from his dream. But that was only half of her.

The right side of the queen's face was a withered husk of flesh the purplish-blue color of a well-aged bruise. An eldritch fire burned in the hollow socket where her right eye should have been.

The two aspects of the queen's appearance were in perfect balance, divided equally down the center of her body.

"Kneel," Ratatosk hissed at ABE and Pru.

They did. ABE was grateful for the excuse to drop his gaze, though some part of him longed to look at the queen again.

"Ah, guests. What a pleasant surprise." The queen's honeyed voice reached out from the throne and caressed his ears. "Two mortal children and the Allfather's pet rat. And look! One of the mortals is my young hero. I bid you welcome. You may rise."

ABE stood, whispering reassurances to Ratatosk, who had not appreciated the rat comment at all. Beside him, Pru rose, too.

"Tell me," the queen went on. "What brings you to my hall?"

"We, ah, were hoping to see Baldur," Pru said.

"I see." The queen considered. "Of course you may see him, then. First, though, you must be hungry. It's been such a long journey. Come. Eat from my plate."

The queen pointed to a table beside ABE. Had it been there when they entered? He hadn't noticed it.

On the table sat a plate covered with succulent meats and fruits so plump and fresh looking that ABE's mouth watered.

Suddenly, he was *famished*. How had he not realized it until that moment? His stomach was empty. He felt like he'd never eaten before! Even the meats looked irresistible—and he was a vegetarian. He reached toward the plate.

"ABE, no!" Pru hissed.

At the same time, Ratatosk dug his claws into ABE's shoulder and whispered. "No! Her plate is hunger. Take nothing. Look away!"

ABE froze, his fingers inches from a juicy-looking apple. He'd come so close to disaster! He lowered his hand to his side.

"No?" the queen said. "Pity. Shall I send for Baldur, then? Nothing would please me more than to give you the gift of an audience with the fallen god."

"Wait," ABE said, interrupting Pru before she could answer. "That's . . . very kind of you. But we aren't looking for a gift . . . as generous as that is. Is there any other way we could speak with Baldur?"

"Such a clever lad." The queen smiled. "And so polite. Very well, young hero. You have pleased me with your good manners. Not a gift, then. We shall make a trade. Truths for truths. I will ask you three questions, which you will answer truly. In return, you may ask Baldur three questions, which he will answer truly. Nothing is taken, nothing is lost. Agreed?"

"Ratatosk?" Pru said.

The squirrel hesitated. "And we may go when we are done?" he asked the queen.

"So long as you abide by the terms of the bargain, yes. I swear on my throne."

Ratatosk nodded.

"Okay," Pru said. "Ask away."

The queen turned to ABE and said, "I think you will find my questions easy. Recently, I delivered a riddle to you. I only wish to see that you showed me honor by giving my words due consideration. Here, then, is my first question. To whom do I refer in my riddle?"

ABE frowned. That wasn't the kind of question he had expected. He glanced at Pru, who nodded encouragement.

"Odin," ABE said. "The truth-teller is Odin, the soothsayer."

"Oh, *very* good," the queen said. "Next. My riddle posed a question. What is the answer to that question?"

"'When is a truth-teller not telling the truth?'" Pru said, repeating the riddle's question. "When he's wrong," she answered.

The queen looked at the two of them, considering. ABE held his breath. Finally, the queen said, "Acceptable. Not the answer I expected, but a valid one."

"What was the answer she expected?" Pru whispered. ABE wondered, too. But he didn't have time to give it any more thought before the queen asked her third question.

"The riddle was a message and I was the messenger. But for whom did I deliver the message?"

"Your father, Loki," ABE said, pleased that he had figured out the true meaning of the riddle.

“Ah,” the queen said. She sounded disappointed.

But was that a good thing or a bad thing?

“Very well,” she continued, and ABE breathed a sigh of relief. “A bargain is a bargain.”

The queen waved her arm, and a column of mist rose from the undulating ground cover. The mist parted and revealed a new seat to the queen’s right. In it sat a man. A halo of blond hair framed the noble features of his face, but his eyes had a faraway look, as though he wasn’t aware that anyone else was present.

“What’s wrong with him?” Pru asked.

“Death is a new state for Baldur. He is still adjusting. He will be able to answer your questions, though, and he will answer them all truly. Such is his nature, and such are the terms of our bargain. Ask.”

“Well, we might as well start with what we came for,” Pru said, looking at ABE. When he nodded, she addressed Baldur. “Do you know who killed you?”

Baldur opened his mouth to speak. Before he could, the queen reached over and lightly rested her hand on Baldur’s arm.

“Answer only the question they asked,” she counseled, “but answer it truly.”

Baldur’s lips thinned—a quick flash of emotion on his otherwise placid face. But he nodded, then said, “Yes.”

ABE waited for more.

"He has to tell us who!" Pru blurted.

"Most certainly not," the queen said calmly—pleasantly, even. "That is not the question you asked. I hope you would not try to cheat me by expecting two answers for one question. Such behavior does not become friends."

"She's right, Pru," ABE said. "We have to be careful—"

"Fine," Pru blurted, "Baldur, *who* killed you?"

"Okay," ABE muttered, "That should work."

The queen's hand remained on Baldur's arm. "Answer her question truly," she said again. Her pinkie finger caressed the fallen god's arm. ABE shivered, thinking about the touch of her rotten flesh.

Baldur closed his eyes and said, "I was killed by my brother Hod, who threw the spear that pierced my heart."

"No!" Pru exclaimed. "We *knew* that. We need to know who gave Hod the spear. Do you—"

"Pru, *wait*!" ABE covered Pru's mouth with his hand and looked at the queen. "That didn't count. She didn't ask a question."

The queen nodded in acknowledgment. The left side of her mouth curled in the smallest of smiles.

"We have to word this question right," ABE said to Pru. "It's our last one."

Pru nodded, and ABE removed his hand from her mouth.

"You'd better ask," Pru said. "You're better with words."

"Baldur, I'm sorry for what happened to you. I hope . . . I hope you're at peace. But we need to know—who gave Hod the spear that took your life?"

ABE hoped that would do it. If Baldur didn't know the answer to the question, he could say so. But if he did know, he would be compelled to tell them who it was.

The fallen god opened his mouth—then closed it again. Strain showed on his face. He looked to the queen.

"You *must* answer their question. And you must speak the truth."

Baldur nodded.

The hall fell silent in anticipation. It was a pure silence, a quiet more still and lifeless than any ABE had ever experienced—the silence of the grave. When Baldur finally spoke, his voice seemed to boom. In truth, though, he spoke softly, a whisper from the dead.

"The trickster."

CHAPTER 21

"INTERESTING," THE QUEEN SAID SOFTLY.

ABE barely heard her.

That was it.

They were done.

They'd solved the mystery.

Throughout most of their investigation, ABE had not just believed that Loki was guilty—he had *wanted* Loki to be guilty. The trickster had caused so much trouble. And so, he had wanted to believe Loki was capable of the worst of crimes.

Now that Loki's guilt had been confirmed, though, ABE felt an emptiness in his belly. Partly, he felt bad for Mister Fox. He'd be so disappointed. Mostly, though, ABE felt bad for everyone else, including himself. Loki had killed Baldur. Odin's visions were true. Ragnarok was coming.

Their only hope now was that it would happen in Earth's distant future. Alva's words came back to him: *The end should always come tomorrow, never today.*

"We must go," Ratatosk whispered in his ear, bringing him back to the moment. "It is not wise to linger too long in the company of death. No."

"Pru," ABE said, touching her shoulder. She looked as lost in thought as he had been. "We need to go."

She nodded and addressed the queen. "Thanks for your help. We're going to get on our way."

They bowed, turned, and started for the door.

The Queen of the Dead cleared her throat. ABE and Pru froze.

"I think . . . I think perhaps not." The queen's voice changed as she spoke. It began sweetly but became something that scratched and crackled. It crawled up from behind them, like a thousand spiders scuttling over each other to get from one place to the next. Even as ABE winced at the sound, he realized it made sense that the queen would have two voices, one for each of her aspects.

"What? Explain!" Ratatosk said as all three of them spun back to face the queen.

"You may go, Messenger," the queen said, her voice once again soft as silk. "I would not keep Odin's pet from his work. But I think the mortal children will stay. They belong to me now."

"No way!" Pru said. "We had a deal!"

"We did," the queen agreed. "One you broke."

"How?" ABE asked, running through their interview with Baldur in his head. What had they done wrong? "We made a trade. We gave you three answers in return for three answers."

"Ah," the queen said. "I see the confusion. It is a simple misunderstanding on your part. Our bargain was not for answers. It was for *truths*. I gave you three. You gave me only two."

"What are you talking about?" Pru said.

But ABE saw it. Too late, he saw how cleanly they'd been trapped. He faced the queen.

"Loki didn't give you the message for me, did he?" he asked.

The queen bowed her head.

"What? Who did, then?" Pru asked ABE.

"I don't know, but it's the only question we could have gotten wrong."

"So we got it wrong! That's not the same as lying!"

ABE shook his head. "Don't you see? It doesn't matter. Not to her. It's like Mister Fox said. Someone can say something thinking that it's right. But if it's not—if it's wrong—then it's not technically *true*. They haven't told the truth."

"A fact you acknowledged yourselves when you answered my second question," the queen reminded them.

"We said a truth-teller isn't telling a truth when he's wrong," Pru said, recalling their answer. Her face paled.

"And I accepted your answer."

"No, no, no!" Ratatosk leapt from ABE's shoulder to Pru's and stuck his head out at the queen. "You're cheating. Deceiving! Defrauding!"

"Watch your tongue, *rat*," the queen said, leaning forward in her throne and showing her first sign of anger. "My bargain was true. *I* am the injured party here. These children gave me two truths and tried to escape with three, in turn. That final truth is a gem of knowledge they did not have when they entered my hall. I cannot allow them to take such a treasure from me. The Queen of the Dead keeps what is hers!"

The queen settled back in her throne. As she did, a low growling sound came from the shadows behind her. An enormous black hound, roughly the size of a small horse, stepped out of those shadows and into the gray light of Niflheim.

"If you disagree," the queen continued, her fractured mouth twisting in a crooked smile, "you may take it up with Garm. Such a precious creature. He *so* hates to see his mistress wronged."

Garm, the hound of the dead. ABE had read about

him. The beast sat beside the queen's throne, his black eyes lost in the deeper night of his fur.

"You can't do this." Ratatosk shook with anger—and also, probably, fear of Garm.

"It is done. Leave now, Messenger, while you can."

"What about ABE and me?" Pru said. "What are you going to do with us?"

"Do?" The queen's voice registered surprise. The hostility of the tone she'd used with Ratatosk disappeared. "Nothing, child. You are my guests. You have my permission to roam my palace as you wish. If you try to leave, however, you will be at Garm's mercy."

"Garm knows no mercy. None! Zero! Null!" Ratatosk said.

"True." The queen folded her hands on her lap, apparently content to sit back and let the two of them decide their own fate.

"What are we going to do?" ABE asked after he, Pru, and Ratatosk stepped away from the queen to talk things over.

"What choice do we have?" Pru said. "We have to stay here for now. Ratatosk, go to Mister Fox and tell him what's happened. He'll figure something out."

"But what can he do?" ABE asked. "He can't leave the Henhouse."

"No. But he's smart, ABE. And he won't abandon us here. You know he won't."

"Yeah. You're right."

"I don't like this, no. Not at all!" Ratatosk said, pulling on his tail. "Death should not be so bold."

"We'll be fine," Pru said.

ABE marveled at her confidence. She had to be scared, too, but she was doing a much better job than he was at appearing calm.

Then again, she didn't know everything he did. His conversation with Mister Fox returned to him, and a fresh worry struck him: how long could they stay in Niflheim before they started forgetting home?

Ratatosk muttered something about the queen that ABE couldn't quite hear. It seemed to have something to do with odor and personal hygiene. He had muttered it *very* softly.

"Fine!" the squirrel said in a louder voice. "I'll be back."

With that, Ratatosk leapt to the ground and fled the room. ABE watched the squirrel go, abandoning Pru and him to Death.

ABE groaned, wishing he hadn't thought of it in quite those terms.

CHAPTER 22

ABE AND PRU WANDERED THROUGH THE TOMB-LIKE PASSAGES OF THE PALACE of the Dead for what felt like hours. ABE couldn't really judge the passage of time in Niflheim. The world of the dead was still, unmoving and unchanging.

Somehow, that stillness was the worst part. ABE felt like he was already a ghost haunting the silent, empty halls of the palace. Only Pru's company and the knowledge that Ratatosk and Mister Fox were working on an escape plan made it possible for him to fight down the panic that built with every step.

Early on, Pru had insisted they scout the gates—just in case. As soon as the palace's exit came into view, however, Garm had seeped out of the shadows.

"Going somewhere?" he'd asked in a low growl.

"You can talk?" ABE had asked.

Saliva had spilled from Garm's mouth, where his red, raw tongue hung over jagged teeth. "Talk. Stalk. Hunt. I do many things, few of them pleasant. Care to learn more?"

They'd left immediately.

Eventually, they found what appeared to be an empty banquet hall and sat in two of the chairs that surrounded the long table.

"Pru, what if we never get out of here?" ABE said, no longer able to hold in his worry. He raked his hands through his hair. "What if we're stuck here forever? What will we do? What will we eat? We don't even know where the bathrooms—sorry, *lavatories*—are and—"

"*ABE*," Pru said, sharply. "Stop it. You're panicking. We can't panic. Mister Fox *will* get us out of here. Then we'll join the search for Loki. We'll see to it that he gets caught and imprisoned for a long, long time."

"You don't know that. You can't!" ABE sucked in his breath, ready to launch into a new list of worries. He was interrupted, though, by another voice.

"Pru? ABE? Are you there?"

ABE bolted to his feet, looking for the source of Mister Fox's voice. Pru was quicker. She dug into her bag and retrieved her looking glass.

"Mister Fox," Pru said. "It's about time!"

"Sorry. I didn't want to reach out until we had a plan for getting you out of there."

"Do you? Have a plan, I mean?" ABE asked.

"I think so."

"I *told you*," Pru said to ABE. "Okay, let's hear it."

"Absolutely. But first—did you talk to Baldur? I have to know! Did he tell you who gave Hod the spear?"

"He did," Pru said. "I'm sorry, Mister Fox. It was Loki."

The detective disappeared behind his hat as he ducked his head. In a way, ABE was glad to be spared the look of disappointment he knew must be showing on Mister Fox's face.

"Okay," Mister Fox said when he finally looked up. "We'll deal with that later. Right now, let's get you two out of there. The plan Ratatosk and I came up with isn't ideal, but it will have to do. I've been searching through the Henhouse for information on Niflheim and the queen's palace. I never spent much time there myself when I was younger. But between my research and Ratatosk's impressive knowledge of the three worlds, I think we've come up with a way to get you out."

"I hope it's not through the front gate," ABE said. "Because, trust us, that's pretty well guarded."

"I heard that you met Garm. Is he as big and mean looking as I remember?"

"Yes!" ABE and Pru said together.

"Well, then I have good news and bad news. Good news first. I have maps here at the Henhouse that suggest that the queen's palace abuts a series of caverns and tunnels that were once mined by dwarves. According to what Ratatosk and I have pieced together, these caverns and tunnels link the three worlds."

"How is that possible?" ABE asked. "I thought Yggdrasil was the only thing that connected the three worlds."

"Yes and no. Yggdrasil is the axis that binds them all together. But Asgard and Niflheim are planes of existence. All Worlds of Myth are, really. And there are places where they touch and overlap. Theoretically, you should be able to escape Niflheim and return to Earth through the caves."

"*Theoretically?*" Pru said.

"Ratatosk knows the entrance, but he isn't familiar with the tunnels themselves. He's clever, though. He'll find the way. He's already on his way back to you. You'll escape together."

"You mentioned bad news," ABE said.

"Right. From what we can tell, the dwarves called the entrance to the caverns Gnipa Cave."

"What's so bad about that?" Pru asked.

"Norse myths associate Garm with two specific

locations. One location is the gate at the entrance to the Palace of the Dead."

"What's the other location?" ABE asked, though he knew what the detective was going to say before he said it.

"Gnipa Cave."

✳

Ratatosk returned a short time later. ABE had never in his life been so happy to see a squirrel.

"Are we glad to see you!" he said. He had to put his hands behind his back to keep from wrapping Ratatosk up in a bear hug—or squirrel hug.

"Yes, yes. Now shush, shortwits, and follow me. We must be quick."

ABE waited for Ratatosk to offer other words for *quick*, as was his usual style. But he didn't say anything else. Instead, he led them from the room. The squirrel's restraint spoke volumes about how dangerous their situation was.

The palace walls proved no match for Niflheim's mist. The vapor had conquered the palace's defenses and infiltrated the corridors as they crept through the darkened halls.

ABE felt better now that Ratatosk had returned and they had a plan. He also felt better knowing that Mister Fox could contact them through their looking glasses. He'd forgotten all about that in his panic about being trapped. Now he walked with the polished handle clenched tightly in his fist. He noticed Pru had her glass out, too.

Every time they came to a set of stairs, they went down. The corridors were increasingly timeworn and decrepit the further they went. The topmost levels of the queen's palace had been made of carefully chiseled stone. The bottommost corridors, though, appeared to have been carved into and through the rock of the mountain itself.

Ratatosk picked up his pace as they approached an intersection of two hallways. "We go left here. Then straight on to the cave entrance. Then up, up, up."

ABE felt his pulse quicken. They were so close!

They turned left where Ratatosk had indicated. The corridor extended straight, its end lost in shadows. ABE squinted and tried to make out the cave's entrance.

Instead, he saw something move in the darkness.

Jagged white teeth flashed into view as Garm emerged from the shadows and said, "Going somewhere?"

No! They'd almost made it. It wasn't fair!

Ratatosk sucked in his breath. His tail ballooned to twice its size as hair stuck out in all directions.

"Let us pass," Ratatosk said. His voice sounded feeble, even to ABE.

"Be careful, Ratatosk," Pru cautioned.

“Oh, I don’t think so, rat,” Garm said. “I think you’ve had your freedom for too long while I’ve been bound to this realm. I think your running days are done. I think *all* your days are done. You first, rat. *An appetizer before the main course!*”

With a vicious bark, Garm lunged toward Ratatosk, knocking ABE to the ground as he raced past him. Ratatosk scampered up the nearest wall and buried himself in a shallow crack in the stone, just out of Garm’s reach.

“Leave him alone!” Pru shouted. She ran at Garm and swung her looking glass at the hound’s head. Garm saw her coming, though, and ducked the blow. He launched himself forward with his hind legs, crashing into Pru’s chest and sending her tumbling to the ground. Her looking glass flew from her hand and skidded into the shadows.

ABE regained his feet in time to see Garm glowering down at Pru.

“Pru, get up!” he called. But she lay on her back looking dazed. Before ABE could think of what to do, Ratatosk leapt from his perch and landed on Garm’s haunch. Grabbing the massive hound’s tail he bit down—hard!

Garm yelped in pain as Ratatosk jumped to the ground. The hound spun on him, his head held low and a wicked growl rumbling from deep in his throat.

"I will make you suffer for that, rat. Your death will be long and slow and oh-so-very-*very* painful."

"Catch me first," Ratatosk said, and he took off down the hall—away from the entrance to Gnipa Cave.

Garm crouched, preparing to give chase. But just before he launched himself at Ratatosk, he stopped. His muscles relaxed and he turned back—slowly—to face ABE and Pru.

"Do you think I am such a fool as to let my mistress's prizes escape? The rat will get his due in time. First, I shall deal with both of you."

Garm moved toward them, malice in his eyes. ABE had managed to get Pru to her feet, but she was still dazed.

He backed away from Garm, pulling Pru along with him. What could they *do*? They could run for the cave, but what was the point? Garm was playing with them now, a cat stalking a mouse. Or maybe a dog stalking a cat. Or, given Garm's size, a horse stalking a . . .

What did horses stalk?

ABE shook his head. It didn't matter! They'd never make it to the cave. Garm would be on them in a second, and then . . .

ABE didn't want to think about what would happen then. He knew it would involve those teeth—those awful, sharp teeth and his and Pru's soft flesh and—

The sound of a small throat clearing halted both

Garm's attack and ABE's rambling inner monologue. The hound looked back, and as he did, ABE saw that Ratatosk had returned.

The squirrel sat calmly on his back legs in the middle of the tunnel. He looked Garm squarely in the eye. Then that insane, rude, wonderful squirrel did what he did best—he started talking.

Ratatosk had spent his entire life carrying messages. ABE didn't know how old Ratatosk was, but the squirrel had to be at least a thousand years old if he'd been around during the days of the Vikings. ABE suspected he was much, much older than that. Most of the messages Ratatosk had delivered had been insults passed back and forth between Nidhogg and the eagle that lived at the top of Yggdrasil. That meant that Ratatosk had been collecting insults over hundreds, probably thousands, of years.

Nothing else could have prepared Ratatosk to unleash the extraordinary verbal assault he delivered at that moment. The astonishing litany of scathing brickbats that emerged from the squirrel's mouth was of such an awe-inspiring and prodigious caliber that even frost giants from the coldest realms of Jotunheim would have felt the heat of embarrassment and blushed. After about a minute, ABE had to cover his ears. Pru lasted a few seconds longer, then she slapped her hands to her head, too. Garm's own ears shot up and a low whine escaped his throat as Ratatosk released a torrent of insults the likes of which had never been heard in the three worlds before and never would be heard again.

A moment of silence followed Ratatosk's tirade. Then Garm's ears curled back against his head and, with a rabid howl, the hound of Niflheim charged the squirrel.

Ratatosk was already on the move, though. He raced down the hall away from ABE and Pru and once more away from the mouth of Gnipa Gave. This time, Garm followed the squirrel, his only thought to retaliate against the abuse he'd received at Ratatosk's hand . . . or, rather, *mouth*.

Two words echoed back through the halls as Ratatosk and Garm disappeared. They were spoken by Ratatosk, his voice hoarse from exertion.

"Run, shortwits!"

CHAPTER 23

ABE HAD THE FORETHOUGHT TO GRAB A TORCH FROM THE WALL BEFORE HE and Pru ran into the darkness of Gnipa Cave. Pru was still a little dazed from Garm's attack. Just how dazed wasn't clear until they'd gone a good ways into the cave and Pru suddenly stopped them.

"My looking glass! I left it back in the palace!"

"Pru . . . we can't go back. I don't know how much time Ratatosk bought us. But I don't think we'll get this chance to escape again."

"I know!" Pru bit down fiercely on her lip, clearly torn. "But do we even know where we're going? We were supposed to escape *with* Ratatosk. He was going to lead the way."

She had a point. ABE craned his neck to look in both directions, unsure what to do. Should they go forward and away from Garm? Or should they go back and find Ratatosk?

In the end, they decided to go on a little ways. So far, the tunnel had been straight, with no side passages. They reasoned they could safely continue for a while. That way, they could put a little more distance between themselves and Garm, but Ratatosk would still be able to find them without any trouble if he doubled back.

The tunnel continued fairly straight, with a slightly upward slope, for a good distance. Eventually, though, their luck ended as the tunnel forked.

"Which way?" ABE asked. "Or do we wait?"

"I think we have another problem." Pru pointed at their sputtering torch.

He'd noticed the dimming light a while ago and had been trying to convince himself that it was his imagination. The thought of the torch going out filled him with uncontrollable fear. They would be entombed in the pitch-dark caverns of Niflheim and left to wander in an endless, empty void for the rest of their lives with no hope for—

Suddenly, ABE's looking glass lit up and an image appeared.

"ABE! ABE, can you hear me?"

"Mister Fox!" Pru exclaimed.

ABE held up his looking glass. Mister Fox's image looked out at them. "Good! You're both there! I worried when Pru didn't respond."

"Things went sour," Pru said. She went on to explain their encounter with Garm, their separation from Ratatosk, and the loss of Pru's looking glass.

"Okay. I agree. Things could be better," Mister Fox said. "But let's not worry too much about Ratatosk yet. He's fast and clever. I'm sure he's a match for Garm."

"We have one more problem," ABE said. "Our torch is about to die."

Mister Fox considered that for a moment. "I think I can help with that. I can teach you how to use some of the looking glass's enchantments to capture the light of the torch. But there's a catch. I won't be able to call you again. If I do, it will break the charm and you'll be left in the dark."

ABE hated the idea of being cut off from the detective. He was sure Pru felt the same way. But the thought of being left alone in the dark was even more terrifying. As it was, ABE was already beginning to imagine he could hear things in the emptiness around them. He'd become aware of a rhythmic tapping sound in the distance, for example. He knew it was probably something natural, like dripping water, but his imagination had partnered with his fear and given birth to all kinds of unpleasant alternatives. Many of those alternatives involved things with very big and very sharp teeth.

"Teach us how to capture the torch's light," Pru said. She looked ABE. "Agree?"

"Yeah," he said.

"All right. But since this might be our last chance to talk for a while, we need to establish a plan. Listen. It's possible Ratatosk won't make it back."

"But you said—" ABE began.

"I know what I said. And I still hope he'll find you. Wait a little while. According to the lore, Garm is bound to the Palace of the Dead. He can't go beyond the palace gate or the mouth of Gnipa Cave. So he won't be able to reach you where you are. But you can't stay forever. If Ratatosk doesn't return—"

"But you still think he will, right?" ABE interrupted.

"If Ratatosk doesn't return," Mister Fox repeated, "you'll have to go on without him."

"How are we supposed to do that?" Pru said, her confidence cracking. ABE felt a fresh burst of worry. "This cave system could be huge. We might never find our way out."

"You don't need to find your way out. You just need to cross the border from Niflheim to Midgard. The Henhouse will note your crossing and take me as close to you as it can. I can use my looking glass for the rest. I *will* find you. Just keep going up."

"Okay," Pru said, sounding a little reassured.

"But you *do* still think Ratatosk is coming, right?" ABE said quickly. "Right?"

"I hope so, ABE. But your torch is dimming. We can't put this off any longer. I'm going to break the connection. When I do, ABE, I want you to hold your looking glass up to the torch so that the mirror is reflecting its light. Then say *zapomni*. Repeat that."

ABE did, and when Mister Fox was satisfied he'd said it right, he continued.

"Good. Then say *pokazhi*."

Mister Fox had ABE practice that word, too.

"Good," the detective said. "Those words will allow you to use some of the looking glass's most basic enchantments. The first incantation will tell the looking glass to capture the image in the mirror. The next incantation will allow you to summon the image. When you don't need the light anymore, say *khvatit*. That will stop the spell."

"Wait," Pru said. "I just thought of something. Why don't we just keep the connection open with you. There's light coming from the Henhouse. That way, we can have light *and* be able to talk to you."

"I considered that. But the looking glasses only work so long before they need to be recharged. That's another purpose of the miniature Henhouses I gave you. Capturing the light will use much less magical energy than keeping this connection open. I'm going to go now before the torch dies. Good luck."

"Wait," ABE said, though he didn't have any good reason other than not wanting to lose the lifeline to the detective.

It was too late. The image in the looking glass faded to black.

They were alone.

Pru nudged him. "ABE, quick!"

"Right," ABE said. He handed the torch to Pru and turned the mirrored side of his looking glass to the torchlight and said, "*Zapomni.*"

"Cross your fingers," Pru said.

ABE did so. His hand shook as he repeated the second incantation they'd been taught. *"Pokazhi."*

Immediately, his looking glass began to glow with a golden light.

"Cool!" Pru said. "Instant flashlight."

"Okay," ABE said, taking a deep breath. He felt oddly reassured by the glowing light of his looking glass. Had he just done magic? Despite their circumstances, a shiver of excitement ran up his spine. He really *did* feel like a wizard.

"So now we wait," Pru said.

They waited.

And waited.

Long after their torch died and they were left with only the faint glow from ABE's looking glass, they waited. Long after they reached the terrible point of certainty that no help was coming, they waited, unwilling to admit to each other that something must have happened to Ratatosk.

As they waited, ABE paced in circles while Pru sat in front of his looking glass where it lay faceup on the ground, like a dim campfire.

What should they do? Part of ABE wanted to still wait for Ratatosk, both because he wanted the squirrel to be okay and because he didn't want to risk finding their way through the caverns without him.

Another part of him, though, was desperate to get moving. How long before they started to forget about their lives on Earth? He kept testing himself to see if he remembered everything about his home and family. But how could he tell if he had forgotten something he didn't remember if he couldn't remember what he'd forgotten?

That thought sounded crazy even to him.

"ABE," Pru said finally, rising, "we have to face it. Ratatosk isn't coming."

"Yeah. I know." ABE stood still. "Do you think he's okay?"

"I hope so. But even if something did happen to him, I think our best chance of helping him is getting to Mister Fox."

ABE nodded.

"ABE, do you hear that tapping sound?"

"I do. It's been going on for a while. I thought maybe it was just in my head."

"No. I hear it, too. It seems to be coming from the left path. I think we should go that way. It goes up at least."

It was as good a plan as any. And it was somewhat comforting to have Pru sound so confident. ABE led the way, his looking glass held before him. The glass provided some light, but the rough and uneven floor of the tunnel demanded their attention.

The tapping sound grew louder as they went. It wasn't as steady as ABE had first thought. It came in starts and stops.

"Hold on a second," Pru said, putting a hand on his shoulder.

"What is it?"

"Up ahead. I think there's another light."

"Maybe we should turn ours off and check."

Pru nodded her agreement and ABE whispered, "*Khvatit.*"

The tunnel instantly darkened. It didn't go pitch-black, though. Pru had been right. There was a faint light ahead of them. A way out?

"The tapping has stopped," Pru whispered.

ABE listened. He couldn't hear it anymore, either. In its place, though, came a new noise: a soft muttering sound.

"There's someone up ahead," he said.

They crept forward until ABE felt Pru's hand on his shoulder again. He stopped, and together they peered around a corner.

Ahead of them stood a short, stout man. His face and hands were black with dirt, and his leather tunic looked old and work worn. Oddly, though, and in stark contrast to his otherwise disheveled appearance, he wore necklaces and bracelets of gold inlaid with gems.

The man ran one hand along the rock of the tunnel wall. The gesture looked strangely like a caress. With his other hand, he lifted a pickax and began tapping the wall, pressing his ear close to the rock as he did. Other tools lay on the ground at his feet.

"What's he doing?" Pru asked in a whisper.

"He looks like he might be mining. Pru, I think he's a dwarf."

ABE had meant to whisper. In his enthusiasm, though, he spoke more loudly than he'd meant to. The dwarf dropped his small hammer immediately and drew a sword from his belt.

"Who's there?" the dwarf demanded.

"Nice, ABE," Pru hissed.

"Sorry."

"Step into the light so I can see you. Slowly, now."

They stepped around the corner. ABE raised his hands in the air until he realized that a Mythic from Niflheim would have no idea what the gesture meant.

"Children! What are children doing in the caverns of Niflheim?"

"Trying to get out, actually," ABE said.

"Out? Go out the same way you came in." The dwarf cocked his head and peered at them. "How *did* mortal children get in, hmm? You're not dead, are you? You don't look dead."

"No. We're not dead," Pru said.

"We're lost," ABE added.

"Lost?" The dwarf gave a hearty laugh. "Yes, I'd say you're very lost! Go on. Tell the truth. How *did* you come to be here?"

ABE had been excited about the prospect of meeting a dwarf. He'd always loved the stories of them toiling in their deep caverns, crafting magical items in their secret forges. All in all, though, he was finding his first actual encounter with a dwarf far less magical than he'd hoped. Judging by the guarded answer Pru gave to the dwarf's question, she felt the same way.

"We probably came in the same way you did," she said. "How did *you* get here?"

"Oh, that's good." The dwarf said. "You're clever, girl."

"Thanks," Pru said.

"I don't *like* clever." The dwarf jabbed his sword in their direction. "Mortals are clever when they're hiding things. What are you hiding, eh? What have you found? Is it gold? Is it gems?"

The dwarf's eyes began to shine with a manic light.

"No, we haven't found anything! We were just trying to get away from . . ." Pru bit her lip.

"Oho! Get away from who?"

ABE looked down at his feet. A quick glance out of the corner of his eye at Pru showed her doing the same.

"Go on," the dwarf urged. "Tell the tale true. We're all friends here. Aren't we?"

"Friends don't usually point swords at each other," ABE said.

The dwarf uttered a sound that was half grunt and half laugh. The covetous look that had taken over his face when he thought ABE and Pru were hiding treasure vanished at least, and he lowered his sword (but didn't sheath it).

"There. See? We're friends. I'm Fadir. Now, tell me. How did you get here?"

"I don't see that we have much choice," ABE said to Pru.

"Okay, fine. I'm Pru. My friend ABE and I came to Niflheim to talk to Baldur. He's dead. Did you know that?"

"What do I care for a god's death?"

"But Ragnarok is coming," ABE said.

Fair shrugged. "Ragnarok has always been coming. All things die. You still haven't told me who you're running from."

"The queen," Pru admitted. "She didn't want us to leave after we talked to Baldur."

"Fleeing the Dark Queen? The queen only keeps what is hers. You are thieves!" Fadir raised his sword again. "What did you steal, hmm? Something beautiful? Something precious? Show me!"

"No, we didn't take anything," ABE said.

"She said we had taken knowledge and that we couldn't leave," Pru added.

Fadir looked disappointed at first, but his eyes quickly lit with greed. "I bet the queen would pay a hefty ransom to see her pretties returned to her."

"No," Pru said. "Wait. Please. We can't go back. We have to get out and get home. Help us."

"And why should I help you?"

"Because . . ." Pru faltered.

"What if . . . what if we pay you?" ABE said.

"You said you hadn't found any gold," Fadir said suspiciously.

"No, no gold. But we have . . ." ABE did a quick inventory, but he knew he really only had one thing to offer. He took out his looking glass and held it out with a sigh. "I have this. It's magic."

"ABE, no!" Pru said as Fadir stepped forward and grabbed the device.

"We want to get out of here, right?"

Fadir ran his hands over ABE's looking glass, paying careful attention to the raven's head carved into its base and muttering all the while.

"Well crafted, yes. And strong enchantment . . . very strong . . . witch wrought!" Fadir's eyes lit up.

"Will that do?" ABE asked.

"All right, boy. Yes. This will do. For this prize, I will show you the way out."

"Great!" Pru said. "How long will it take?"

"Not so fast. The witch glass buys the boy's safe passage. What do *you* offer?"

"What? That's not fair. I don't have my looking glass anymore. I lost it."

Fadir shrugged. "No payment, no bargain."

Desperately, Pru began to dig through her satchel.

"What's that?" Fadir asked, suddenly alert. "Something metal. I can smell it."

Pru frowned. "There's nothing . . ."

Fadir dropped ABE's looking glass into a leather pouch and grabbed Pru's bag with the hand that wasn't holding his sword. He dropped her bag to the ground and reached inside. When he withdrew his hand, he held Pru's dad's badge.

"Hey!" Pru said, taking a step forward, "That's mine."

"This is valuable, is it?" Fadir clutched the badge to his chest.

"No. It's not even real gold. Now give it back!"

"No, not gold, but still valuable," Fadir said, studying Pru. "Or why would you want it so much, hmm? Yes, very valuable, I think. Give me this, and Old Fadir will return you both to Midgard, sure enough."

Pru opened her mouth to object but then closed it and held her tongue. ABE saw her inner struggle in her narrowed eyes and chewed lips.

"*Fine*," she said at last.

"Pru, are you sure?" ABE knew how important the badge was to her. Was she agreeing to give it up because it was her only choice? Or was she beginning to be influenced by their time in a World of Myth? Would she be able to live with her decision once they returned home?

"It's fine, ABE. So it's a deal? You'll get us out of here and return us to Midgard in return for our treasures?"

"Perhaps." Fadir studied them. He raised his sword again. "Or perhaps I'll just *take* the treasures."

"You don't want to do that," Pru said, backing away.

"No? Why?"

"Because . . ." Pru paused, then her eyes lit up, "because, like you said, the looking glass is witch wrought. We have magic. If you take our stuff, we'll put a curse on it *and* you."

Fadir hesitated. "You have no power."

"No? Show him, ABE."

ABE blinked in confusion. Show him? Show him what?

Pru gestured with her eyes to Fadir's bag.

"Oh!" ABE said. He raised his arm in what he thought looked like a wizardly gesture and said, "*Pokazhi.*"

ABE's looking glass flared to life and Fadir's pouch began to glow.

Cursing, the dwarf dropped the pouch and stepped away.

"Peace!" he said. "No need for that. It was a jest. We're friends, remember? I'll take you away from the queen."

"And take us to Midgard?" Pru pressed.

"Yes."

"We have your word?"

"Yes!" Fadir hissed.

Pru nodded to ABE.

He raised his hand again and waved it through the air.

"*Khvatit.*"

CHAPTER 24

THEY WALKED IN SILENCE. ABE DIDN'T MIND. THEY'D BEEN TRAVELING UPHILL almost from the start, and his muscles were beginning to ache. He wasn't sure he had the breath to spare to talk.

That thought gave him pause. He remembered his and Pru's journeys in Asgard. They'd never tired there. And he hadn't felt tired when they'd started their climb with Fadir. If traveling through Worlds of Myth didn't drain a person, did the fact that he was getting tired mean they were getting close to Midgard?

Maybe. He couldn't be sure, though. Anyhow, he had other concerns. Thirst and hunger soon outweighed the soreness in his legs. His lips felt dry. He passed the time as they walked seeing how long he could wait before moistening them with his tongue—and then how long it took for them to feel dry again.

When they came to a somewhat level and open area where the tunnel forked, Fadir said they would stop for a rest. ABE collapsed against a rock. Pru did the same a few feet away.

"You don't have any food, do you?" she asked ABE.

"No. I wish I did."

They both looked at Fadir.

"Not my job to feed you," he said as he stacked a few bits of kindling he'd pulled from his pack.

"You said you'd get us out," Pru said. "You're breaking the bargain if we starve to death."

"You're not going to starve to death." Fadir began striking two stones together. Sparks jumped from the stones to the kindling.

"No, but if we're weak from hunger and slip on the next climb, it's the same thing. So give us our stuff back if you're not going to feed us. Unless *you're* the thief."

Fadir glared at Pru over the blossoming fire. The lighting transformed his face into a mask as craggy as the rocky tunnels around them. Pru held his gaze. After a moment, Fadir reached into his pack once more and pulled out a large chunk of bread. He broke a piece off and threw it to Pru, who in turn broke some off and handed it to ABE.

"I suppose you'll be wanting water, too," the dwarf said.

"If you wouldn't mind," ABE said.

Fadir threw him a leather flask and ABE took a few swallows. He handed it to Pru without drinking as much as he would have liked. Pru didn't hesitate. She took a long swig before handing the skin back to Fadir.

Silence settled over the small camp at that point. ABE was tired, but he couldn't make himself comfortable enough to sleep. After a while, the silence became too heavy. Normally, he would have trusted Pru to break it. But one look at her made it clear that she was still angry with Fadir for taking her father's badge.

"So . . . I guess it's lucky we found you," ABE began.

"There's no luck, boy, no chance. Only fate."

"Right. So, um, what were you doing in the tunnels? Looking for gems? Not that I'm prying!" ABE quickly added. "I'm just trying, you know, to make conversation."

Fadir grunted and tended the fire. "There's treasure in the tunnels below. Most are too frightened of the queen to search for it."

"The other dwarves, you mean? Where are you from? Nidavellir?"

"So the human boy knows something of the dark fields?"

"Only from the stories I've read."

"And what do *you* know about stories, boy?"

It was an honest question, so ABE answered it honestly. "I know they change with the telling."

Apparently, the answer amused Fadir. He gave a bark of laughter.

"Well, then you know more than most. But you've only got it half right. They change with the telling, yes, but they change more with the teller."

"How so?"

The glow from the fire lit Fadir's face from below, casting him in an eerie light. His eyes glinted as he peered at ABE through a veil of smoke that rose from the flames. The smoke drifted up through one of the two tunnels that climbed steeply away from their camp.

"People tell the story they want you to hear, boy, true or not," the dwarf said.

ABE considered that.

"Enough talk," Fadir said. "It's been a long climb. We'll camp here tonight and go the rest of the way in the morning." The dwarf pulled a rolled blanket from his pack and placed it under his head. His snoring soon filled the cavern.

"Great. He snores, too. What a wonderful traveling companion." Pru pulled her knees to her chest and rested her forehead on them, eliminating the possibility of conversation with ABE.

ABE felt sad for Pru. He knew how much it hurt

her to lose her dad's badge. But he was also relieved to see that she was upset. It meant that they hadn't been in a World of Myth for so long that they'd lost their connection to home.

ABE rolled over. He didn't think he'd be able to sleep. But at some point in the unending, cavernous night, his eyes closed as exhaustion overtook him.

He wasn't sure how long he slept. When he woke up, the fire had mostly turned to ember and ash. It took long moments for his eyes to adjust to the dying light. When he could finally see, he jumped to his feet.

Fadir was gone.

They were alone in the caves.

Then the fire died, and all light vanished from the world.

CHAPTER 25

UNTIL THAT MOMENT, ABE HAD NEVER FELT CLAUSTROPHOBIC. HE KNEW WHAT the word meant, of course.

Claustrophobic: suffering from the fear of small, enclosed places

He'd been in small places before. It had never bothered him. But now he was in a cave somewhere between two worlds. There could be rocks for miles in every direction. He felt them all pressing in on him—crushing him.

His breath became slippery. He couldn't catch it. He began gasping. Hyperventilating? The definition swam through his dizzy mind.

Hyperventilate: to breathe at an excessively rapid rate, often brought on by fear or anxiety

Yes! He was definitely hyperventilating.

He felt a hand on his shoulder. He jumped.

"ABE, it's me!"

"Pru?" His breathing began to slow. It was still dark and he was still scared, but at least he wasn't alone.

"Yeah. ABE, Fadir's gone."

"I know. What are we going to do?"

"To Fadir? Something *really* unpleasant if I have anything to say about it. If we ever see him again, I mean."

"No, Pru, what are we going to *do*? We're alone. Fadir took our only light! We're basically buried alive!"

"I know, ABE. Don't you think I know?"

ABE could hear the fear in her voice. But he could also hear that she was trying to control it. He tried to follow her lead. He forced his breathing to slow even more and tried to think past the terror.

"Fadir said we would finish the climb today," he said aloud, remembering. "Maybe the exit is nearby."

"Maybe," Pru said. "Or maybe he was lying so he could run off on us and steal our stuff. But okay. Let's assume we're close. The tunnel splits in two directions from here. Which tunnel should we take? Fadir never told us."

ABE didn't even want to think about Fadir. He wished he could erase the memory of his last glimpse of the dwarf. Fadir had looked ghoulish in the firelight, wrapped in the rising smoke of the fire.

"Wait! Pru, that's it!" he said.

"What's it?"

"Before the fire went out, I saw the smoke rising up one of the tunnels. I remember it because I thought it made Fadir look creepy."

"Fadir *did* look creepy."

"Well, yeah. That's true. But I thought he looked creepier through the smoke. But the smoke—Pru, It was rising up the tunnel on the left."

"So?"

"It's like smoke going up a chimney in a fireplace. It might mean that there's some kind of ventilation that way."

"So you think that tunnel will take us outside?"

"I don't know. Maybe?"

"Maybe is better than anything else we have."

It wasn't easy making their way in the dark. They crawled so they could feel the ground ahead of them. The uneven floor of the tunnel threatened their hands and knees with sharp corners. Fortunately, the *domovye*-made pants and gloves proved more than durable and protected them as they groped their way through the dark.

ABE felt something tickle his cheek. He paused, waiting to see if it came again.

"Pru," he said, trying to contain his excitement. "I think I feel a breeze."

Pru was quiet a moment. "I feel it, too!"

They crawled more quickly, pulled by the promise of fresher air.

"ABE . . . am I crazy or is it getting brighter?"

He blinked, almost too afraid to trust his eyes. An excited giggle escaped his lips. It sounded ridiculous, but he didn't care!

"It is! It *is* getting brighter. Pru, I— OUCH!"

ABE's knee hit a rough piece of rock. Wincing from the pain, he reached out to find its edge. It rose up from the tunnel's floor and seemed to level off at about a ninety-degree angle. He gasped.

"Pru . . . I think these are steps!"

He heard Pru fumble in the dark. "You're right! They're rough, but they *are* steps. I think we found the exit!"

They clambered up the steps using their hands and feet. It was *definitely* brighter than it had been, and when ABE looked up, he saw a rectangular break in the darkness ahead, like an open entryway. They abandoned all caution and scrambled upward. ABE began to hear a roaring sound. In the dark, confined space of the tunnel, he couldn't tell if the sound was coming from somewhere nearby or if it was the sound of the blood rushing in his ears.

They burst, gasping for breath, through the opening at the top of the steps and emerged into an enormous cavern. Staggering into the wide-open space, they turned in a slow circle trying to figure out where they were.

Once on vacation, ABE's dad had taken ABE and his mom to a huge indoor football stadium. The circular cavern he and Pru discovered at the end of their climb out of Niflheim could have held two of those stadiums with room to spare. The domed ceiling was broken in the center by a large round opening, through which ABE could see both the moon and a heavenly assortment of stars.

Most of the cavern's light came from that opening far overhead, but not all. There were gems of various sizes visible in the walls throughout the cavern. The gems somehow captured and amplified the moon's light, filling the space with a magical silvery glow.

ABE lowered his gaze to the smooth floor of the cavern. With a start, he realized the roaring sound he had heard in the tunnel wasn't the blood rushing through his ears. A river cut through the center of the cavern, running from east to west.

"ABE, look!" Pru grabbed his arm and pointed to the eastern wall. ABE gaped in astonishment.

Two stone towers jutted out from the wall of the cavern. They rose from the floor to the ceiling, as tall as skyscrapers with a wide-open space between them. One tower stood on the north bank of the river, the other stood on the south bank, where he and Pru were. A number of bridges connected the structures, crossing the river at various heights along the towers.

"It's a dwarvish outpost!" ABE said. "It looks abandoned."

"Does it?" Pru pointed again, and ABE saw what he had missed. One of the windows near the bottom of the tower on the northern side of the river shone with light. It flickered like the open flame of a campfire.

"Do you think it's Fadir?" he asked.

"I don't know who else it could be. Let's find out!"

"What? Pru, no! We're almost out." ABE inhaled deeply. The cool, fresh air made him feel almost giddy. "I can see the sky!"

"I know, but unless you can fly, we have no way of getting up there. And look around. There are *dozens* of tunnels leading from this place. If we go the wrong way, we could end up more lost than before."

She was right. There had been so much else to see that he hadn't noticed the other tunnel entrances that dotted the walls of the cavern.

"We can do this, ABE," Pru said, placing a hand on each of his shoulders. "That has to be Fadir. Who else could it be? He'll know the way out. And even if he refuses to help us, we'll *still* be okay. That's the moon up there. *Our* moon. We're back on Midgard. That means that Mister Fox is on his way. I don't just want to stand around waiting for him."

He was so tired. But she was right. They were already exhausted and starving. They were probably dehydrated, too. Fadir had supplies, and he would know the way out. There was no telling how long it would take Mister Fox to find them.

"Okay," he said, taking a deep breath. "Let's go."

They followed the curve of the cavern wall to the tower, trying their best to stay out of sight. The bridge at ground level had crumbled, forcing them to enter the southern tower and climb to one of the bridges higher up. They found one that looked safe enough to cross on the third level. It was about as wide as a two-lane highway, and ABE stayed away from either edge as they crossed. He didn't much like heights.

"Wow," Pru said, stopping midway across the bridge. She pointed. "Look."

"Wow is right," he said, following Pru's direction. He'd assumed that the towers were the only structures in the cavern. They weren't. The gap that separated the towers stretched back into the wall, rising from the river to the ceiling to form a *huge* tunnel, large enough that the Statue of Liberty could have walked through it, if that were something she were inclined to do.

On either side of the gap, all along the north and

south walls of the tunnel, were more towers and spires. They stretched back as far as ABE could see.

"It's not a dwarvish outpost," he said in an awed voice. "It's a whole underground city."

"It's pretty amazing," Pru said, "but it's not what we're here for. Come on."

ABE pulled his eyes from the magnificent city of stone and followed Pru the rest of the way across the bridge.

The northern tower was in a much worse state than the southern. The ceiling of the first chamber they entered had caved in, covering its only other exit with a pile of rubble and timber. Fortunately, they were able to scramble up the pile to reach the level above, though they had to move carefully.

Their caution paid off. Had they been moving more quickly, they might not have heard the sound of a voice as it rose up through the floor of a nearby room. They crept into the adjoining space and found a narrow crack in the corner of the floor. Light shone through the crack. ABE and Pru moved closer and peered through the tiny opening. A figure crouched over a fire in the room below.

ABE had expected it to be Fadir. They both had.

It wasn't.

It was someone else ABE recognized, though, and perhaps the last person in the world he expected to see.

Loki.

CHAPTER 26

THE LAST TIME THEY'D SEEN HIM, LOKI HAD LOOKED PRINCELY. NOW his torn clothes hung loosely on a body covered with grime.

He was talking to himself. His mutterings echoed off the rock walls.

"Not long. Not long. They'll find me. He'll tell them how, when it suits him." He wrung his hands together over the fire. "Where to go? Where to run? Nowhere! I'm trapped. I can take any shape, but always Loki. Always the villain."

ABE felt a tap on his shoulder, and he looked up to see Pru gesturing toward the exit. Tiptoeing, ABE followed her to a spot a safe distance away.

"How is that even possible?" Pru said. "What are

the odds that we show up in the same cavern Loki is hiding out in?"

ABE tried to reason it out. "Maybe it does make sense—sort of, anyway. These caverns go down to Niflheim. The queen is Loki's daughter. Maybe he thought he could escape down there if he needed to. I wonder why he's stayed here, though. He looks like he's seen better days."

"He's going to see worse," Pru said, her lips set in a firm line.

"What do we do now? Should we—"

The room grew darker as the light coming from the cavern dimmed. Clouds must have covered the moon. A muffled wail rose up from below.

As quickly as they could manage while still being quiet, they returned to the spyhole and peered down. Loki had moved out of sight. Before they could decide what to do, he burst back into view, tugging his hair.

"Found! I'm found!" Loki stomped out his fire and disappeared into darkness. His voice remained, though, muttering over and over, "What to do?"

Pru and ABE tiptoed back to the next room to talk.

"It's Mister Fox," Pru said. "It has to be!"

"Do you think that he saw the fire? Do you think he's on his way?"

"I don't know. We have to get him here. Quick, go

back to the bridge. Get his attention in case he didn't see the light."

"I can't leave you here!"

"I'll be fine. I'm just going to keep an eye—or ear—on things. If Loki leaves, I might be able to see where he goes."

ABE didn't like it, but he agreed.

He found his way back to the bridge and stood in the middle of it. He scanned the cavern. His knees wobbled a bit as he saw three figures racing across floor. Not only had Mister Fox found them, he'd brought Thor and Hilde, too!

ABE waved his arms like a wild man. He resisted the urge to shout, and instead took his jacket off and began swinging it through the air. That seemed to work. He saw Mister Fox grab Thor's arm and point. They'd seen him!

ABE gestured toward the door in the southern tower where he and Pru had entered. Mister Fox and the others headed off in that direction, and ABE soon lost sight of them. He ran the rest of the way across the bridge to meet them, fighting back the urge to laugh. He couldn't believe it! They were rescued! And Loki was nearly caught.

Mister Fox appeared first. Hilde followed and Thor came last, a barely contained storm of energy.

"ABE! Thank goodness you're okay," Mister Fox said. "Where's Pru?"

"She's fine. She's back keeping an eye on Loki."

"Loki?" Thor exclaimed.

Hilde turned to shush him. "Can you take us to him, boy?"

ABE nodded. "Follow me."

They had nearly made it across the bridge when Pru poked her head out a window. Her short bob of hair framed her face.

"It's no use sneaking!" she called. "He saw you coming. He leapt into the river and shape-shifted into some kind of fish!"

"As my father foresaw!" Thor bellowed, turning on his heel. "To the river!"

ABE hesitated. Something was wrong. "Mister Fox, there's—"

"Not now, ABE. We have to catch him!" Mister Fox shouted. He grabbed ABE's sleeve and dragged him back across the bridge. When ABE tried to protest, the detective hissed in his ear, "Not here."

When they reentered the southern tower, Mister Fox called on the others to stop.

"There's no time!" Thor said.

"Wait!" Mister Fox insisted. "Go on ahead. But leave me a net."

"Why?" Hilde asked.

"A hunch," Mister Fox said.

"Give him what he wants," Thor said, already descending to the level below.

Hilde opened her shoulder pack and handed Mister Fox a folded up piece of mesh.

ABE paced, troubled.

"It was her hair," Mister Fox said as Hilde disappeared after Thor.

ABE stopped. Her hair? Of course!

"That wasn't Pru who poked her head out of the window," ABE said, catching on. "It was Loki. He took her shape, but he made his hair too short. He made it look like it did when he met Pru last year."

"Loki must be panicked. He wouldn't normally miss a detail like that. Let's make that work in our favor. Loki is going to be watching the river to see if we take the bait. He'll be focused on the others, especially Thor. If we're lucky, you and I can cross the bridge while he's distracted. Come on."

Keeping as low as possible, they raced across the bridge once more. ABE started to lead Mister Fox to where he'd left Pru, but Mister Fox stopped him. The detective was surveying their surroundings with his looking glass.

"This way," he said.

Mister Fox moved like his namesake. They wove their way through a labyrinth of rooms and corridors

ABE hadn't seen before. But Mister Fox's instincts were true. He paused when he reached a particular chamber and gestured that ABE should stop, too. They peered through a crack in the door.

Loki stood inside with his back to them. He was looking out a window, presumably watching Thor and Hilde. ABE couldn't see Pru anywhere.

Mister Fox pulled out the small piece of mesh Hilde had given him and began to unfold it. It was a finely woven net, so thin ABE doubted it could hold anything. He wondered if it was magic.

It certainly turned out to be larger than ABE had first thought. When Mister Fox was done, he and ABE held a net that was easily large enough to catch a man. Mister Fox mouthed, "Ready?"

ABE nodded.

"On the count of three." He paused. "One . . . two . . . three!"

They burst through the door. Loki spun around the moment they entered. He was fast. Feathers sprouted from his arms. His face narrowed and his nose became beak-like.

"Now, ABE, throw the net!" Mister Fox yelled.

ABE did. Mostly, he just released the net and let Mister Fox do the throwing. It settled on Loki before he could complete his transformation. Entangled, Loki fell to the ground with a thud and reverted to his true form.

ABE looked desperately around the room. He found Pru bound and gagged in a corner. He raced to her and crouched down to untie her.

"I was almost done!" she shouted as soon as her gag was removed.

Looking down, ABE saw Pru had found a sharp rock and begun to cut through the ropes on her own. He fell back to a sitting position. She was amazing.

"Are you okay?" Mister Fox asked, joining them. "Can you walk? Because we have to leave here. Now. Before it's too late."

CHAPTER 27

"WHAT DO YOU MEAN, 'BEFORE IT'S TOO LATE'? WE CAUGHT LOKI!" PRU SAID. "It's over."

ABE studied Mister Fox. A tightness remained around the detective's eyes.

"Yes, we caught Loki," Mister Fox said. "Now let's go fetch Thor and Hilde. The net was made by the goddess Ran. It will hold Loki and keep him from changing shape until they can collect him."

With the attention turned back to him, Loki ceased his struggles. "Do not do this to me. I beg you."

"Why, Loki?" Mister Fox crouched beside him. "Before we go, I have to understand. *Why?* The last time we crossed paths, you were trying to change your fate. Why did you surrender to it?"

"Surrender?" Loki cried. "I did not surrender to my fate. It conquered me!"

"That's not an answer!"

"I have no answers!"

Loki twisted so that he faced Pru.

"Pru," he pleaded. "We were friends once, when I was Fay."

"You were never Fay! You were lying to us the whole time."

"No! I was kind to you." Loki shifted to look at ABE. "Wasn't I always kind to you?"

"You were going to let Gristling kill us!"

"Only when I had no choice! I tried to let you go. Do you remember? Do you truly think I would have forgotten you in Asgard? I saw your escape. *I let you go!*" Loki writhed in desperation.

"Enough!" Mister Fox snapped. "This isn't about last year. This is about Baldur."

"And I am innocent! I did not kill Baldur! Listen to me. I beg you!"

"We don't have any more time for lies. Pru, ABE, we're leaving." Mister Fox gave Loki one last, inscrutable look. Then he rose and started for the door. Pru and ABE followed him. Loki shouted after them.

"Listen to me! I am innocent! *LISTEN TO ME!*"

It wasn't until they were across the bridge and halfway down the tower, with Loki's cries for mercy still echoing behind them, that Mister Fox said, "The sad part is, despite everything, a part of me still wants to believe him."

"Where's the Henhouse?" ABE asked, wanting to change the subject and spare Mister Fox the embarrassment of being wrong. "I didn't see it when you arrived with the others."

"It's hundreds of miles from here, in the nearest graveyard I could find. That's why I had to call on Thor and Hilde. I didn't have any choice. I needed their flying ship, *Skidbladnir*, to get here."

"They have a flying ship? Sweet!" Pru said.

"Where is here, anyway?" ABE asked. "I didn't think there were any caves around Middleton."

"What makes you think we're near Middleton? We're in Norway."

"Seriously?" Pru said.

"Become a Fibber," Mister Fox said. "Travel the world. Meet interesting deities. It's all part of the job description."

Pru gave a nervous but excited laugh. ABE wanted to be excited, too. But there was something beneath Mister Fox's humorous tone that worried him.

They reached the bottom of the tower and exited into the vast cavern. In the distance, Thor and Hilde walked along the river, searching the waters. Each held a net.

"Over here!" Mister Fox called to them, waving. "We caught him. *Hurry!*"

"What's the rush?" Pru asked. "You said the net would hold him."

"It's not the net I'm worried about." Mister Fox scanned the cavern as though expecting someone. "Where's Ratatosk, by the way?"

"Ratatosk never came back," Pru said. "ABE and I had to make our own way. We met a dwarf, Fadir. He led us here. Well, he led us most of the way here, the creep. ABE had to give him his looking glass, though. And I had to give him my dad's badge."

"You met a dwarf?" Mister Fox stopped his examination of the cavern long enough to look at them. "In all the vast expanse of the caverns around Niflheim, you found a dwarf who led you here, to this spot?"

Thor and Hilde arrived then, and Mister Fox, frowning, turned to them.

"Loki's caught, neat as you please, in a net in the north tower. Just follow the desperate screaming. You'll be getting my bill posthaste. All checks should be made out to *The Unbelievable FIB*. In the meantime, Thor, why don't you put those big, brawny shoulders to use and collect Loki *so we can leave*."

Thoom . . . Thoom . . . Thoom.

Mister Fox stiffened.

ABE spun around, trying to discover the source of

the sound seeping into the cavern. A number of the tunnels leading to the space, all of which had been dark just a few moments before, now blazed with a fierce red light.

Thoom. Thoom! THOOM!

The sound didn't seep anymore—it poured into the chamber. It was a rhythmic banging, like that of a thousand drums beat in unison, or the sound of a marching army. Light shone in even more of the tunnels now, more than ABE could count. But it was the shadows newly visible in the lighted tunnels that sent ABE's voice soaring to its highest pitch. Shadows invaded the cavern, shadows of shapes huge and small, some with too many heads and arms.

"What's happening?" ABE cried.

"Mister Fox?" Pru said, pulling on the detective's sleeve.

"Too late," Mister Fox whispered, spinning in a slow circle. All the blood had drained from his face. He looked like a ghost. "They're here."

"Who's here?" ABE asked.

"Think about it," Mister Fox said, his voice uncharacteristically flat. "Some of these tunnels connect Earth and Niflheim. But there are other realms close to Niflheim, realms touched by Niflheim's cold and cruelty."

“What realms?” ABE asked, afraid he already knew the answer.

“The coldest reaches of Jotunheim,” Hilde said.

“That means . . .” Pru didn’t finish the sentence.

Thor did.

“Frost giants.”

CHAPTER 28

"THIS IS LOKI'S DOING," HILDE SAID, DRAWING HER SWORD. "HE BAITED US and now the trap is sprung."

"Loki!" Thor roared, launching himself in the direction of the tower where Loki lay. "I must retrieve him!"

Pru started after him, but Mister Fox grabbed her arm.

"Let him go, Pru."

"What? But Loki . . ."

"Is Thor's problem. We're leaving! But which way?" Mister Fox scanned the cavern.

"Why don't we just leave the same way you came in?" ABE asked.

"There *has* to be another exit."

There wasn't. Every single tunnel now glowed red. They were surrounded.

"Here they come!" ABE cried, pointing.

The first frost giants charged into the cave through a tunnel on the other side of the river. They weren't alone. Trolls ran alongside them, like rabid dogs at the giants' heels, brandishing vicious spiked clubs. The frost giants wielded swords and axes that burned with the reflected light of their torches.

"We don't have any choice," Mister Fox said. He thrust his looking glass into Pru's hand. "Take this. You'll know what to do with it when the time comes. Now we have to move. There! See where the river exits the cavern? That's the way. Go!"

"Why are you giving me your looking glass?" Pru asked. But the detective ignored her question and pushed her into motion.

They ran. ABE and Pru did their best to keep up, but they were tired from their escape from Niflheim and Mister Fox had to adjust his pace. The distance stretched on forever as they ran toward the river's exit through the west wall of the tunnel.

More giants and trolls soon joined the first arrivals. An endless tide poured into the cavern, threatening to cut off their exit. The monsters' stampede sounded like thunder.

No. Wait.

That *was* thunder!

Thor had emerged from the tower with Loki slung over his shoulder. Seeing him, the swarming mass of monsters shifted course. ABE watched in astonishment as Thor grew in size and clashed with the first of his attackers.

Then ABE, Pru, and Mister Fox reached the west wall of the cave. There they found an ancient and narrow dwarvish road that ran alongside the river through a tunnel in the cavern wall. The road rested just below an embankment and only a few feet above the water level of the river.

The surface of the road was wet and slick. ABE barely managed to keep his footing as they raced along. The echo of the river's roar buffeted them in the enclosed space of the tunnel, blending with the clang of the battle that had begun behind them.

Theirs was the one tunnel from which no monsters had emerged. ABE soon saw why. This tunnel did not lead to a mythical realm. It led outside to fresh air and skies that had once been clear but that now roiled with the thunder god's battle rage.

"We're in the mountains!" ABE exclaimed, taking in the snowcapped peaks all around. Beside them, the river exploded out of the tunnel and plunged hundreds of feet down before disappearing into a cloud of misty spray.

They stood on a stone platform that had been built into the mountain by the dwarves, long ago. In addition to the road they'd followed from the cave, another path led to the southeast, back along the outside of the mountain.

ABE scrambled back from the precipice and pressed himself against the hard rock wall. A gust of wind threatened to rip him from his perch. His knees nearly buckled as he imagined it pulling him to the edge and over and down . . . and down and down.

"We have to keep moving," Mister Fox said. "We don't have any other choice. Maybe if we're fast enough . . . *come on!*"

The detective led the way along the stone path. ABE tried to keep his eyes fixed on Mister Fox's back. He looked over the edge of the path once, though—and immediately wished he hadn't. They were hundreds of feet up. A fall would mean certain death on the rocks below.

"*Travel the world,*" Pru said behind him, repeating Mister Fox's words from earlier. "*Meet interesting deities . . . all part of the job description.*"

ABE nodded, swallowed, and fixed his gaze on Mister Fox's back once more.

The path gradually grew wider. They reached a stretch where they could easily have walked side by side with room to spare. Mister Fox hurried ahead, though. Pru followed next as ABE struggled to keep up.

CRACK!

The deafening sound tore through the air, and the whole mountain shook. ABE stumbled back a few paces and fell to all fours.

"What was that?" Pru cried, also on her hands and knees.

"The mountain!" Mister Fox said, leaning against its side for support. "The dwarves hollowed it out too much. It can't take the punishment Thor and the giants are dishing out. The mountainside might as well be an eggshell—it has about as much chance of holding up against the battle going on inside! We need to get out of here!"

ABE and Pru never even got the chance to stand up.

CRACK-A-BOOM!

The next tremor, ten times more powerful than the first, shook ABE's bones and rattled his teeth. He looked up just in time to see a huge boulder come crashing down from above. It was heading right for Pru!

"Pru!" he shouted, reaching for her. But he was too far away to help.

Pru couldn't scramble to her feet fast enough. She'd be crushed!

At the last moment, somehow, Mister Fox appeared.

He shoved Pru to safety, then staggered back as the boulder crashed down and came to rest on the ledge between them, blocking the detective from view.

"What was that?" Pru said, recovering. The detective's looking glass had slipped from her hand and skidded across the ground.

"It sounded like the whole mountain split in two. Actually, I think maybe it did," ABE said, pointing to the wall of rock above them. A vertical fissure had appeared in the side of the mountain, just next to the boulder that had nearly crushed Pru. The fissure was large enough to drive a tank through.

"It doesn't sound like it's stopped, either," Pru said. Rumbling continued to fill the air, sounding a little more removed than before. "It sounds like the whole cavern's collapsing. I bet that crack goes all the way back to—wait. Where's Mister Fox?"

"He's on the other side of the—*PRU, LOOK OUT!*"

ABE's warning came too late. A shape appeared in the crack in the wall, a fearsome and giant-sized shape that might have been conjured from ABE's worst nightmare. Gristling erupted from the fissure.

"At last!" Gristling bellowed. "He told me that if I brought my clan and my allies to this place that I would see both of you again. *Finally, I will have my vengeance!* And I shall begin with you, girl!"

Pru tried to get up and escape but cried out in pain

and fell back to the ground, grabbing her ankle. Roaring in triumph, Gristling reached for her.

"Gristling!" ABE shouted.

The giant lifted his head, and ABE locked eyes with the monster. Even with the bruises, even with the wound on his cheek that left the giant's wild beard caked with blood and grit, ABE knew Gristling's face. It had haunted his days and his dreams for the past year. It had been a burden of fear that ABE had carried for too long. He was sick of the burden. He was sick of Gristling's face. So he would banish it.

ABE lifted his arm. He held Mister Fox's looking glass.

"*NO!*" Gristling shouted as ABE caught the giant's reflection in the enchanted mirror and transported the monster back to the frozen reaches of Jotunheim.

"ABE!" Pru shouted. "You did it!"

ABE stumbled to her side. "Are you okay? Your ankle—"

"I'm fine," Pru said, standing. She winced, then leaned on his shoulder. "Well, mostly fine. I think I might have sprained my ankle. It's not bad. It just surprised me. Come on! We have to get to Mister Fox."

ABE returned the detective's looking glass to her and together they edged their way between the boulder and the mountain. ABE could feel the mountain still trembling beside him.

When they emerged on the other side of the boulder, they found the ledge empty.

"I don't understand," Pru said. "I thought you said he was over here."

"He was. I saw him. He stumbled back away from the boulder and . . ."

The same thought struck them both at the same time. They rushed to the edge of the ledge and looked over the side.

CHAPTER 29

ABOUT TEN FEET BELOW ABE AND PRU, MISTER FOX CLUNG TO THE MOUNTAIN. His hat was lost to the unforgiving ground hundreds of feet below, and his hair blew freely in the wind. One arm hung limply at his side.

"Mister Fox!" Pru cried.

"Are you okay?" ABE said, then felt instantly foolish.

"Climb up!" Pru said.

"I can't." Mister Fox's voice was laced with pain. "The boulder clipped my arm. My shoulder's dislocated. The arm may be broken."

"ABE, we have to save him!"

"I appreciate the sentiment," Mister Fox said, "but you have to go."

"Are you insane? We *will* save you," Pru said. She coughed, probably choking on all the dust created by the shuddering mountain. There were tears in her eyes, too, though ABE didn't think they were from the dust.

"There's no time. You have to go."

"I won't leave you!" Pru dropped to her chest and stretched her arm down as far as it would go. "I won't let you go!"

"Letting go. That always is the hardest part."

"ABE, find something," Pru cried. "Some rope—something! *Please!*"

ABE scrambled up and scanned the area for anything that could be of use. A vine, maybe. There was always a vine in the movies. Why couldn't this be the movies?

"What are you talking about?" Pru said, turning her attention back to Mister Fox.

"Letting go. Sending Fibbers out to Worlds of Myth. Wondering if it's right. Wondering if they're ready." The detective winced with pain. "Then, when you return, flying off in the Henhouse. It's never as easy as it seems, or as I make it sound."

"What does that even mean?" Pru was sobbing now. ABE hurried back to her.

"There's nothing, Pru," he said. "I'm sorry. I'm so sorry. I don't know what to do!"

A panicked chant rose from the back of ABE's

mind, a variation on what Alva had said to them: *Al-ways tomorrow, never today. Always tomorrow, never today. Please! Never today!*

The mountain shook again.

"Pru, ABE, you two have to go! The cavern is col-lapsing. And it's going to take the whole mountain with it!"

ABE wondered how Mister Fox could know that.

"I won't leave you!" Pru shouted again. "*I won't!*"

"I know," Mister Fox said.

Then he did the only thing he could do, the hard-est thing.

He let go.

CHAPTER 30

ABE LED THEM ACROSS THE TREMBLING GROUND AND THROUGH THE ROCKS that fell like crushing tears. He had to drag Pru at the start—she hadn't wanted to leave the spot where Mister Fox had fallen and vanished from their view, from their lives, forever.

The mountain continued to collapse until there was nowhere left to go. The ledge ahead crumbled before their eyes. They were trapped on the edge of a mountain that was decaying around them like an anthill in a hurricane.

"I'M SORRY, PRU," ABE shouted over the sound of the world falling apart around them. "I DON'T KNOW WHAT TO DO."

Pru clutched Mister Fox's looking glass to her chest

and stared with glassy eyes into the emptiness before them. ABE looked back at the mountain, wondering how much time they had left.

Something burst into view from beyond the mountain's crumbling peak. It flew almost straight up into the air. At first, ABE thought it was an enormous rock—but the mountain wasn't exploding, it was collapsing! It shouldn't be shooting anything into the air.

The object soared into the sky a short distance before its upward climb stopped. It hung in the air a moment, then circled back down. It looked like . . . it was! It was a Viking longship, not unlike the one they'd seen Baldur laid to rest in!

The ship sailed through the air and came to a stop next to the small ledge where ABE and Pru stood. Thor leapt from the vessel, scooped them up, one in each arm, and returned to the ship just as the ledge gave way beneath them.

"How?" It was all ABE could manage to say as Thor deposited them safely on the deck.

"*Skidbladnir!*" Thor said, gesturing to the ship. "A marvel of dwarvish construction. Once its sails catch wind, it can travel anywhere, over sea or land. The god Freyr loaned it to us for our search for Loki. Now, the gray shade, lad. The one you call Mister Fox. Where is he?"

"He . . . fell," ABE said, struggling with the words. "He's gone."

Thor placed a hand, surprisingly gentle, on ABE's shoulder. "Rest, lad. I will see to things."

The thunder god called out to Hilde as he set off across the deck of the ship, but ABE didn't hear what Thor said to her. Exhaustion and grief overwhelmed him, and he fell into a deep sleep. If he dreamt, he did not remember it.

He woke up to find himself wrapped in blankets on the deck of *Skidbladnir*. Pru lay beside him in blankets of her own, still sleeping. Not wanting to wake her, ABE rose carefully and quietly. Every muscle in his body felt stiff and sore. He walked to the stern of the ship, where he found Thor and Hilde.

"Ah, lad, you're awake. Good," Thor said. "How do you feel?"

"Thirsty mostly," ABE said.

Hilde tossed him a leather skin.

"Thank you," he said after a long drink. The water helped him feel more alert. "Where are we? How long have we been traveling?"

"We are near your town, lad. *Skidbladnir* travels fast. It is nearing the middle of night. Before we return you to your home, though, there is a matter we must discuss." Thor stepped aside and revealed Loki, still wrapped in Ran's net and now wearing a gag. "Loki's fate must be decided."

"Throw him overboard."

ABE turned, startled at the sound of Pru's voice. She stood behind them on shaky legs. Even in the moonlight, ABE could see her eyes were red.

"Pru!" ABE said, alarmed as much by her words as her appearance. "We can't . . ."

"It's his fault Mister Fox is dead! He brought those giants. He killed Baldur and Mister Fox. He is going to kill *everyone*. He needs to be punished!"

"You are not alone in thinking so," Hilde said with a grim nod.

"He cannot die," Thor said. "Even if there are those who think he deserves it."

"Why?" Pru demanded.

"Ah, now we get to the heart of things." Thor drew a hand across his face. His fingers traced through his long, unruly beard. "It is time you knew the truth. You see, my father first met Loki long ago, before he drank from the Well of Wisdom. My father prized Loki's clever mind. They became fast friends. Many were their trials and travels. In time, they took the Oath of Brotherhood. They shared blood and were bonded. On that day, Odin vowed that no one in Asgard would ever bring any harm to Loki. That is why, in part, Loki has never faced any consequences from the gods for his misdeeds. That blood oath my father gave protects Loki from all types of retribution."

"Wait—does that mean you can't punish him?" ABE asked. "Then what has this all been for? Why even bother to capture him?"

"You are correct, lad," Thor said. He hooked his thumbs in his belt and looked down at the deck of the ship. "We cannot pass judgment on him . . . but you can. Loki's actions on Midgard last year leave him vulnerable to your judgment."

"Great!" Pru said. "He's guilty!"

"I misspoke." Thor faced ABE. "*You*, lad, have the authority to pass judgment on Loki."

"What?" ABE staggered back. "Me? Why me?"

"Because Loki took you from your home last year. Prudence went to Asgard by choice to save you, her friend. A noble act. But you had no choice, lad. Loki took you. He trespassed into Midgard and stole you from your home. By rights, you can make claim against the trickster. You, and only you, can judge Loki guilty of evil acts. Doing so will give the gods the freedom to imprison and punish him on your behalf."

"But . . ." ABE didn't know what to say. He didn't want that power.

"It is a heavy burden," Thor said. "I wish it were not ours to place on you, or yours to bear."

A memory rose up in ABE's mind. "The day I met

you at Winterhaven house, you were shouting at someone before you came into the room. You were yelling at Odin, weren't you?"

Thor nodded. "I do not like that we gods cannot resolve this on our own."

"Wait," Pru said. "So the only reason you came back to Middleton was because you needed ABE?" Pru said. "You didn't think I—we—could help you find Loki. You just needed ABE here to pass judgment."

"None of this has any bearing on the here and now," Hilde said, interrupting. "We can wish forever that things were different. It changes nothing. Loki is caught. The boy must pass judgment."

All eyes turned to ABE.

He stared back at them, trembling. Why was he so scared? He knew Loki was guilty. Their investigation had proved it. But a lifetime of indecisiveness bore down on him. Why did *he* have to choose? What if he was wrong?

He shifted from foot to foot, and for once did not force himself to stop.

Could he refuse?

The thought came to him in a rush. What would that do to Odin's vision of the future? Would it change things? Maybe it would even stop Ragnarok!

As if he'd read ABE's mind, Thor spoke. "If we do not act, lad, the end will come now. You saw the giants and trolls rally to Loki's side. It was good fortune and the strength of Hilde's and my own arm that allowed us to escape with Loki from that cavern. If Loki goes free now, he will bring Ragnarok today."

"And if we imprison him?" ABE asked, seeking reassurance.

"The gods of Asgard existed for thousands of years before encountering your people in Midgard. Loki's imprisonment could last for thousands more. I do not know."

All they could hope for was time. *Always tomorrow. Never today.*

"Do it, ABE," Pru urged. "He's guilty. You know he is! Baldur said so. And think of what he did to you last year. He has to be stopped!"

"I know," ABE whispered.

"Then what say you, lad?" Thor asked in a low, somber voice, the last rumblings of a passing storm.

"GUILTY."

ABE's judgment hung in the air. No other words were needed. Thor nodded, and ABE withdrew.

The rest of the journey passed in silence. Pru and ABE sat in the aft of the ship. They were too tired to talk.

Skidbladnir came to a rest against the cliffs alongside the Fort of the Fallen in Middleton. A walkway unfolded from its port side and settled on the grass outside the fort. Another time, ABE might have marveled at the ingenuity of the mechanism by which the walkway appeared. That night, he couldn't be bothered. He followed Pru off the ship. Grief left little room for long good-byes, and soon *Skidbladnir* sailed off into the night.

"It's done," ABE said.

Pru didn't say anything. She just limped toward home. ABE followed, thinking about how different things felt this time compared to their last homecoming. He soon learned how right he was.

They first realized something was wrong in the short stretch of road that connected the fort to the town. Pru walked with downcast eyes, so ABE was the first one to notice the flashlight beams crisscrossing through the woods. The voices came next, people calling his name and Pru's.

A flashlight blinded him, and he heard a voice he didn't recognize shouting "Here! Here, I've found them! Over here. They're okay!"

Almost instantly, he and Pru were surrounded by people asking if they'd been hurt. Someone put a blanket around ABE's shoulders and guided him and Pru to a fallen log, encouraging them to sit down.

Slowly, ABE's exhausted brain started to put together what had happened. Somewhere in their trek through the tunnels of Niflheim to the dwarvish city, they had crossed the boundary between Niflheim and Midgard. At that point, time had begun to pass normally. He and Pru had been gone from home all night and day. They'd returned somewhere in the early hours of the second night!

The town had organized a search to help find the two missing children. A part of ABE felt flattered. Mostly, though, he was embarrassed by all the attention.

More and more people gathered around them, checking on them and handing them water. ABE heard someone say they looked exhausted and dehydrated. He supposed they were. He found himself with a bottle of water in each hand and three more bottles on the ground at his feet. A drop of condensation rolled onto his hand from one of the bottles. It reminded him of standing before the windows at Winterhaven House. How many days ago had that been? Two? Three? So much had happened.

People stepped aside as a police car slowly pulled to a stop in front of them, its lights flashing but without the siren screeching. ABE thought he recognized the man who got out as Pru's dad's old partner. ABE's dad was with him.

"She's right here in front of me, Annie," Roger Lyons said in the cell phone he held to his ear. "ABE's with her. Yes, they both look fine. No, no. Don't come down. I'm going to bring them both to Middleton General, just to get checked out. Meet us there. Yes, I swear they look okay."

"ABE!" his dad said, grabbing him in a rough embrace. Was his dad crying? His dad never cried. ABE hadn't thought he knew how. "Are you okay?"

"I'm fine, Dad," ABE said. Somehow, his dad crying seemed more surreal than everything else that had happened since their journey to Niflheim.

People stepped back to give Mr. Lyons room to approach. ABE noticed Pru was still clutching Mister Fox's looking glass. He thought for a moment that perhaps he should hide it, but then realized that nobody except Pru and him could see it, anyway.

Mr. Lyons knelt down in front of them. "You two gave us a scare. Are you okay?"

ABE waited for Pru to answer. She just stared ahead.

"We're okay, sir," ABE said. "Sorry to scare you."

Mr. Lyons's worried eyes lingered on Pru a moment before focusing on ABE. "What happened, son? Did you get lost?"

Lost? It made as much sense as anything. Everyone knew he and Pru went for hikes in the woods.

"Yeah. We, um, we went out for a hike. We must have gotten turned around or something. We lost the trail. Then we just seemed to get farther and farther from town. I think Pru sprained her ankle." ABE looked at Pru, realizing that he needed to say something to explain how upset she was. "Pru realized at one point that she'd dropped her dad's badge. She got really upset. We tried to find it. We looked everywhere."

At the mention of her father's badge, Pru convulsed. ABE realized that she was crying silently.

"Oh . . . oh, hey, kiddo, it's okay. It's okay." Roger put his arms around Pru. "It's just a thing. Your dad is still with you. He'll always be with you."

ABE bowed his head. He wasn't sure he'd be able to explain why his eyes were also filled with tears.

CHAPTER 32

ABE'S PARENTS KEPT HIM HOME FROM SCHOOL THE NEXT DAY SO HE COULD rest. When he returned to class the day after, Pru was still absent. When school ended, he went to her house to check in on her.

Pru's mother answered the door when he knocked. She must have taken the day off work.

"Hi, Mrs. Potts. I don't mean to bother you. I just wanted to see how Pru was doing."

"No bother, ABE. I'm glad to see you. Come in." Mrs. Potts stepped aside so ABE could pass.

"Thanks."

"I was actually thinking about calling to see if you'd be willing to come by. Pru's been so upset since getting lost. She barely leaves her room. She hasn't cried like this since her dad. I didn't realize losing his badge would hit her so hard. I think it's just opening up old wounds."

"Yeah. I think loss is hard for Pru."

"You're a good friend, ABE." Mrs. Potts ruffled his hair. "Go on up. I don't know if she wants company. But if she'll see anyone, it will be you."

ABE nodded and made his way to Pru's door.

"I'm not really in the mood to talk right now, Mom," Pru said when he knocked.

"It's, uh, not your mom. It's me. ABE."

"Come in." Pru sat on her bed, propped up by pillows. Mister Fox's looking glass lay beside her. Next to it sat the card she'd received last year, the one that had begun their adventure. It seemed appropriate to have it there, now, at the adventure's end.

"Hey." ABE stood awkwardly by the door. For the past couple of days, he'd wished he'd had someone to talk to about Mister Fox's death. Now, though, he wasn't sure what to say. In the end, he said the only thing he could think of. "I miss him, too."

Pru turned to the window. ABE looked down at his feet. Neither of them spoke for a while.

"He knew it was going to happen, you know."

ABE looked up, startled. "What? Who?"

"Mister Fox. He knew he was going to die."

"*What?*"

"I kept thinking about what he said before the end. Remember? He gave me his looking glass and said I'd know what to do with it. I kept thinking about that. Then I realized I *did* know what to do with it."

Pru held the looking glass out so the mirrored side faced ABE. He stepped forward.

"*Pokazhi*," she said.

Mister Fox's face swam into view in the looking glass. He sat in the Henhouse's library, below the painting of Baba Yaga. For a startled, wonderful moment, ABE thought the detective was calling them, that he had cheated death and that the fox was in the Henhouse once more.

Then what Pru had said sank in. Mister Fox wasn't calling them. The detective had recorded a message on his looking glass the same way ABE had recorded an image of the torchlight. Pru had used the word to summon the image.

"Pru, ABE, if you're watching this, then that means I'm already dead." Mister Fox leaned back in his chair. He offered them his last lopsided grin. "Well, that's morbid, isn't it? Still, you can't say it's inappropriate. I mean, I do live in a house in a graveyard, surrounded by countless household spirits. Death has been waiting for me for a while, I think."

Pru choked back a sob. ABE wondered how many times she'd watched this.

"First things first," the memory of Mister Fox continued. "You two need an explanation. I suspect you're wondering how I could know to send you a message from beyond the grave. It was the Eye of Odin. Do you remember when ABE handed it to me in the cemetery last year? I made the mistake of looking at it. *Into it*. And it looked into me. It showed me the future, my future. It showed me my death.

"The images were quick—scattered flashes across my mind. I saw Loki, captured. I saw a battle in a cavern, an escape onto a ledge. I saw Pru, nearly getting crushed. And I saw . . . well, you know what I saw. If you're watching this, then you saw it, too. And I'm sorry for that. I truly am. I thought . . . I thought perhaps that I could change things. I thought . . .

"That doesn't matter now. What matters now is you two. My story is done, but yours is just starting. Make the stories of your lives be fantastic. Because you two, you're brilliant. It's been the joy of my life to work with Fibbers like you. Because there's one thing so many myths, so many stories get wrong. So often, they tell you that the heroes are special because they're born with some power or because they're from some special lineage. That's not so. True heroes are special because of what they *choose* to do, not what they were born to do. They're special because they're brave, and kind, and clever. You two are those things, and more. You're unbelievable."

In the image, Mister Fox stood, and ABE realized a *domovoi* must have been holding the looking glass, because the view followed Mister Fox as he donned his coat and hat.

"We've arrived in Norway, the *domovye* tell me. You two are miles away yet. Thor and Hilde are on their way to meet me with *Skidbladnir*. It's a flying ship. How fantastic is that?"

The childlike delight that showed in Mister Fox's eyes whenever he was exposed to magic shone brightly as he strode through the Henhouse, down the long hallway of doors that led from the inner courtyard to the exit.

"What's coming next will be hard for all of us. Don't worry about me. I've had a good life. A long one. I've seen wonders most people can't even imagine. And, one could argue, the greatest mystery lies before me. One last question to answer. So don't worry. Be strong. The monsters may be out there, they may be coming, but it's like I told you once before, Pru. There are things that make the monsters worth facing. Traveling houses. Talking squirrels. Brave companions."

Mister Fox paused before the final door of the Henhouse. He looked directly into the glass.

"And you two, Pru and ABE, are among the bravest and the best. Good-bye."

With that, the final door to the Henhouse opened, and Mister Fox stepped out into the light.

"He's gone," ABE said as the image in the glass faded. Tears rolled down his cheeks. "He's really gone."

"That's how come he didn't want to join the search for Loki," Pru said. "He knew what would happen if we found him."

"It explains why he was so desperate to believe Odin could be wrong, too. It wasn't about wanting Loki to be innocent, not really. Or at least not completely. It was about wanting to believe that he could change his fate."

"But he couldn't. And he *knew* that when he came to get us in Norway. But he came anyway."

"To save us," ABE said. Every moment he'd ever doubted the detective came crashing down on him. The guilt threatened to bury him.

"I think I'm going to lie down now," Pru said. "I'll talk to you later. Okay?"

"Yeah. Okay."

Pru returned the looking glass to its spot on the bed beside the card. The side of the card with Mister Fox's handwritten note lay faceup: *Be grave in your search, and avoid having stones in your head.*

That clue had led him and Pru to the cemetery. As he walked home alone, ABE hoped that, wherever he was, Mister Fox was resting in peace.

CHAPTER 33

THAT NIGHT ABE HAD A DREAM.

Or maybe it was a nightmare.

ABE stood once more in the hall of the Palace of the Dead. Baldur was gone. Only the queen remained, perched on her throne.

"You disappoint me, young hero," she said.

"Sorry." ABE ducked his head. Was this just a dream? Or was it another message?

"Are you? Then return to me."

"Um . . . I don't think I can do that."

The queen stood and vanished. ABE took a step back, startled. When he did, he backed into something—or *someone*.

The queen's shriveled right hand settled on his

shoulder from behind. Her dark fingers curled in a vise-like grip, and ABE's skin crawled at the frigid touch. Breath heavy with the scent of rotten things touched his left ear as the queen's voice—the awful, scuttling voice—whispered, "You cheated me. You *stole* from me."

ABE pressed his eyes closed.

"I know. And . . . I'm sorry. I really am. I mean, I know you tried to trick us and everything. But . . . but it was a good trick. And a fair one. We just *couldn't* stay." The funny thing was, he meant what he said. He hadn't liked the outcome, but he had to admire the way the queen had outsmarted them with words.

The pressure vanished from ABE's shoulder. He slowly opened his eyes. The queen sat on her throne once more. Her burning eye held his gaze.

"You speak the truth," she said in her honeyed voice.

ABE swallowed and nodded.

"What a curious thing." The queen folded her hands on her lap. "So be it. Your debt is paid."

"What?"

"I accept this truth as payment. Three truths given, three returned. You and your friend are free of any obligation to me."

"Really? That's . . . wow. Thank you!"

The queen inclined her head. "But you may still

return, if you wish. I would give you a place of honor here, young hero. I think it would surprise you to know that there are some who hunger for my attention."

ABE looked upon the two aspects of death, the beautiful and the terrible, and he felt fear, yes, but comfort, too.

"No. No, I don't think it would surprise me," he said.

The Queen of the Dead raised her eyebrow.

"Another truth. And a kindness. Two things that are rarely given freely, and two things I have known little of. Very well, young hero, I will not be found wanting. Let there be a balance. In kindness, I shall return to you something you lost while in my realm. For the truth you may ask me one question. I will answer it as best as I am able."

"That's very kind," ABE said. "But I'm not sure I have any questions left. Well, wait. Actually, there is one thing I still don't know. If Loki didn't give you the riddle to send to me . . . then who did?"

"Odin," the queen said.

"Odin? I don't understand. Why would Odin send me the message?"

The queen smiled. "I offered you a truth, young hero. I said nothing of the gift of understanding. One does have a reputation to maintain. Farewell."

ABE WAS PLEASED WHEN PRU RETURNED TO SCHOOL THE NEXT DAY. SHE returned physically, anyway. Mentally, she still seemed absent as she went through the motions of the day, lost in her grief.

The other kids mostly avoided them as they walked through the halls. ABE was used to that, though. What he didn't expect were the glances people kept shooting them and the half-heard whispers that carried to his ears. Apparently, his and Pru's disappearance had been the subject of a fair amount of talk. He learned how true that was at the end of the day.

When the bell announced that language arts was over, Mr. Jeffries asked if he could have a word with ABE. Pru said she'd wait for him outside the school.

"ABE," Mr. Jeffries said after she'd left, "I just want to say first of all how glad I am that you and Pru are okay. We were all very worried about you here. Every teacher in the school was out looking for you two."

"I really appreciate that. I know Pru does, too."

"Actually, ABE, it's Pru I wanted to talk to you about. I know that Pru has had a difficult time the last few years. I heard the story about her father's death. It's no wonder that she's been in so much trouble in school. I'm sure she's a good kid. I don't think there are any bad kids. But you're a good kid, too, ABE. Everyone around here says so. Now, I don't know what you and Pru were doing out there in the woods the other day—"

"We just got lost—"

"I know, I know." Mr. Jeffries held up his hands in a placating gesture. "I'm just saying, I'd hate to see you get wrapped up in anything bad, ABE, just because your friends don't always make good decisions. I'm sure you know what I mean."

He did know what Mr. Jeffries meant. And he'd had enough.

"You're wrong," he said.

"Excuse me?"

"You're wrong. And . . ." ABE struggled for words. Pru always made defying authority look so easy. What would she say in his place? "And, sorry, but you're being a jerk."

"Excuse me?"

"Sorry!" ABE winced. "Well, mostly. I know you're not really a jerk. I actually think you're really nice most of the time. And I really like your class. But you're wrong about Pru."

Mr. Jeffries leaned back in his chair and studied ABE. "Okay. I'm listening, ABE. Tell me why you think I'm being unfair to Pru."

ABE took a deep breath. "Ever since school started, you've been suspicious of her. I've seen it. She's seen it. But you haven't really taken the time to get to know her. You made up your mind about her before you even spent time with her. You heard all Mrs. Edleman's stories about how she was a troublemaker, and you let that affect how you thought of her. So every time something bad happened, you assumed she did it and . . ."

ABE stopped, frowning.

"And?" Mr. Jeffries prompted.

"Huh?" ABE blinked. He'd forgotten for a moment that Mr. Jeffries was there. "Um, sorry, Mr. Jeffries, but can I go? I'm sorry I called you a jerk. I am. I'm just . . . it's been a hard week. But I do think you're not being fair to Pru."

Mr. Jeffries was quiet just long enough that ABE began to worry he'd gone too far.

"Okay, ABE. You can go. I accept your apology. And . . . I'll think about what you said."

"Thanks," ABE said. Then he left the room at a near run. He didn't slow down until he'd found Pru outside the school.

"Pru, we have to go to Winterhaven House."

"What? Why?"

"I'll explain when we get there. *Please*, Pru. It's important!"

WINTERHAVEN HOUSE LAY IN RUINS WHEN ABE AND PRU ARRIVED A SHORT time later. News reports after the trolls' attack had claimed that the devastation was caused by a gas leak and explosion. Reporters had celebrated the fact that no one had been hurt or killed. Mister Fox would have called it a reasonable explanation.

People saw what they wanted to see, and they didn't see what they didn't want to.

They entered the remains of the mansion unchallenged and made their way to the long room where they'd twice met with Odin. The room was empty. The table had been shattered. No fire burned in the fireplace.

A huge hole gaped in the room's eastern wall, and

through it ABE saw a short scruff of land that ended in a cliff overlooking the ocean. A single figure stood on the cliff, leaning heavily against a staff. He wore a blue cloak and a broad-rimmed hat. Two ravens circled overhead.

"I've been expecting you," Odin said, staring out at the sea as they approached. "You have a question, boy, yes?"

"Well, yeah. Actually, I do. I've been thinking about Loki—"

"ABE," Pru interrupted, rousing herself from her grief. "I don't want to talk about Loki."

"I know, Pru, but we have to. *I* have to. I got into a little argument with Mr. Jeffries just now. I told him I thought it was so unfair that he made his mind up about you because of things Mrs. Edleman told him. It made me so angry that one person would judge another based on stories they'd heard. But then I realized something. That's just what I'd done—it's just what everyone's done—to Loki."

"Loki is, was, and must ever be evil," Odin said.

"But did it have to be that way?" ABE asked. "I know Loki did terrible things. But people saw him as the bad guy even before he did anything bad. They judged him because of the stories you told. You didn't just let the future happen. You nudged it along by making everyone hate Loki. He told us once how hard it was for him living in Asgard. I don't think he was lying about that. It's almost like you wanted to turn Loki into a villain. But why would you do that, unless . . ."

And, just like that, ABE knew the answer.

"You *wanted* this to happen. Didn't you?"

"What did I want to happen, boy?" Odin challenged.

"This, all of this. I don't know why . . . but it's the only thing that makes sense. You *want* Ragnarok to happen."

"ABE, that's nuts," Pru said. "He dies in Ragnarok. Everyone dies. Why would he want that?"

"Why wouldn't I?"

Slowly, Odin lifted his head enough to peer at them beneath the rim of his hat.

"You pitiful insects. You presume to understand the mind of a god?" Odin slammed his walking stick on the ground. "What do *you* know of the future? Do you think that because you glimpsed a vision in my Eye that you know something of what *I* know? Bah! Your mortal minds could not begin to understand! You saw a hint of the future. Moments. A blink of the Eye. I did not see *the* future. *I saw every future!*"

"What?" ABE asked, stunned.

"I saw *every* future. When I drank from the Well of Wisdom, every possible outcome of every event was laid before me like the infinite branching of Yggdrasil's roots. Each branch represented a different possibility, a different future. *And I saw them all!* Can your tiny human mind begin to imagine what that meant to me, Odin—god of wisdom, seeker of knowledge—to suddenly know *all* things?"

"But . . . if you saw a lot of futures . . . then that means you chose which stories to tell," Pru said. "You chose the future you wanted. ABE was right. You wanted all of this to happen!"

"But you'll die," ABE repeated, staring at Odin. *"Everyone dies."*

"Yes! I will die. Finally! I will die leading the gods of the north in a final, triumphant battle in which evil will be vanquished from the world. They will sing songs of my sacrifice and my triumph until the end of time!"

"You're insane!" ABE said, shaking his head in disbelief.

"No, boy. *I'M BORED!* Your mortal mind cannot conceive my burden. You cannot imagine what it is to be a god of wisdom, always craving knowledge, always seeking answers . . . and then, in one moment, to have all knowledge given to you with one sip from an enchanted well. No more seeking, no more learning. No more questions. Just an eternity of days, *which you have already lived.* No more!"

Odin threw wide his cloak and stood at his full height. He towered above them, casting off the illusion of the tired, world-weary old man.

"Let the god of wisdom die. Let me be Odin, god of war! Father of battles! Odin, the Warrior! Odin, the Terrible! Let the ax age begin! The wolf age! Let the age of blood and battle and death begin!"

ABE and Pru staggered back, cowed by the awesome figure before them.

"You cannot imagine how long I have had to wait for this or how carefully I have planned. I have manipulated each choice and navigated each branch of the future with more skill than that miserable squirrel navigated the branches of Yggdrasil. It began with him, of course. I let him see me bury what you called the Middleton Stone. I knew the wretched rodent was so desperate for attention that he would tell Loki where it was hidden. I used Ratatosk and the stone as bait to lure Loki here to this town so he could meet the two of you."

"But why *us*?" ABE asked.

"When I drank from the Well of Wisdom and had my future—all my futures—stolen from me, I knew that my only redemption would be to die in honor and glory as befits a god of war. And I knew that the only villain worthy of me was Loki. So I turned everyone against him by sharing my visions of his evil deeds. But that was not enough. I knew that for Loki to become the villain I needed, I had to turn him against Asgard. To do that, I needed him to suffer. I needed him punished."

"But you couldn't punish him," Pru said. "Thor told us so. No one in Asgard could punish Loki because you and he were blood brothers."

"Yes. It was a foolish indiscretion of my youth, but it was also an oath I could not break. The magic was too strong. No one in Asgard could punish Loki. So I needed a judge who was not from Asgard. I scanned my memories of the futures I'd seen, searching for the right mortal pawns. They had to be clever enough to keep the Eye from Loki, but easy enough to manipulate into condemning him when the time came."

ABE expected outrage from Pru. Instead, she spoke in a monotone. "You used us," she said. Her shoulders slumped.

"And you both played your parts perfectly," Odin said. "I hid the so-called Middleton Stone here so Loki would follow and cross paths with you both. I saw that he would abduct the boy and that, when the time came, the boy would judge him guilty. Of course, to condemn Loki, you first had to find him."

Odin spun in place, sweeping his cloak about him. By the time he completed his spin, Odin, Allfather of the gods, did not stand before them.

Fadir did.

"It was you?" ABE said. He'd completely forgotten that Odin had the ability to change his shape, as he had in the myth about the Mead of Poetry.

"Of course. Did you truly think it was luck you met a dwarf in the caverns of Niflheim that led you, by chance, to Loki? There is no chance."

"Only fate," ABE said, finishing the now familiar refrain.

"Only *me*," Odin corrected.

Another spin and Odin stood before them once more.

"But take comfort, children. You may disagree with my actions and my motives, but in the end I was right. Perhaps I was hard on Loki. Still, he showed his true colors at the last. He committed an unforgivable act. He killed my son and proved himself the villain. And now you have ensured his just imprisonment. You are heroes."

Were they? ABE didn't feel like a hero. Did Loki's crime justify Odin's cruelty to him? Or did Odin's manipulations *make* Loki commit the crime? Who was the villain? And did it even matter anymore?

ABE had so many questions left in his head.

Pru, it seemed, just had one.

"Why?"

She appeared a bit more alert as ABE turned to look at her.

"Why what?" he asked.

"Nothing. It doesn't matter." Pru's eyes once more lost focus as she retreated.

"No, really. What did you mean?" ABE asked, eager to keep Pru present in the moment.

"I understand that Odin manipulated Loki. But Loki never wanted to be the villain. What changed his mind? *Why* did Loki kill Baldur? It's the one thing we never figured out. We were looking for motive and opportunity. We found out that Loki had the opportunity to kill Baldur. He was in the right place at the right time. But we never established a motive." She shook her head. "Never mind. Who cares? It doesn't matter now."

ABE frowned as Pru turned away.

Why *had* Loki done it? They knew he was guilty. Baldur had told them so.

Except he *hadn't* exactly. He'd said the trickster had killed him. Why had he phrased it like that? Things had been so crazy since their interview with Baldur that ABE hadn't given the god's choice of words any thought. But why hadn't he just indicated Loki by name?

He supposed Pru was right and it didn't matter. Everyone knew Loki was the trickster.

In short, avoid assumptions. They're just beliefs in different clothes. Mister Fox's words echoed in ABE's memory.

But Loki *was* the trickster. He fit the definition perfectly. ABE should know. He'd just defined the trickster figure for Pru a few days ago: Trickster figures are usually able to change their shape. They're also usually greedy. That greed can drive them to cause trouble, but sometimes their actions can bring about good things and be a boon to people, too.

ABE gasped!

Pru looked at him, but without any real interest. It was Odin who spoke.

"Have you figured it out at last? You were close before. I'll grant you that. You figured out that *truth-teller* referred to me. But you never quite got the answer to my riddle right. You see it now, though, don't you? *When is a truth-teller not telling the truth?*"

"When he's a trickster," ABE said as the truth delivered its crushing blow.

The definition of a trickster fit Loki perfectly. But it fit Odin, too. The clues to the riddle were in the myths. Odin had changed his shape in the myth about the Mead of Poetry. *And* he shared the mead with people and gods alike—so his greed also resulted in gifts for humankind.

"It was you. *You killed Baldur!*"

"I did what had to be done."

ABE paled as the horror of the act sank in. *Filicide*, the deliberate act of a parent killing her or his child. It was a definition ABE wished he didn't know.

"But . . . but I don't understand," ABE stammered. "We talked to Baldur. Why didn't he just tell us it was you?"

"My doing, I'm afraid. I foresaw your interview with my son in the Palace of the Dead. I knew you would ask him who killed him. So I whispered a charm in my son's ear at his funeral. It prevented him from naming me as his killer, even in death. Of course, your bargain with the queen forced him to answer your question truthfully. A difficult position. So my son gave the only answer he could. He spoke the truth, but not the complete truth. Not a lie, either. Something in between." Odin's eye shone wickedly. "A fib, shall we say?"

"Don't you *dare*!" Her fists clenched at her sides, Pru glared at Odin. "Don't you dare even talk about him!"

"No . . . but . . . this doesn't make sense!" ABE insisted, hands digging through his hair. He didn't want it to make sense! But it did—all of it, and more. ABE could see everything now. Odin hadn't just had motive—he'd had opportunity, too. He'd *created* opportunity. The myths had offered more clues. Odin had cast the charms that had made Breidablik a safe haven. Of course he was able to bypass them. And Odin had allowed mistletoe to be the one thing that could hurt Baldur. It had been such an obvious oversight! But no one had looked too closely at the holes in the myths because everyone had always assumed Loki was the villain of the story.

Still, ABE didn't understand one thing. "The riddle basically tells us you're the killer. But *you* sent the riddle. Why would you do that?"

"Because my one regret has always been that Loki would be remembered as the clever one. Evil, yes. But clever. But now we know the truth, don't we? You once boasted to Loki, child, that while he was the Lord of Lies, you were the better Fibber. Perhaps so. But now we three know the truth. I outsmarted you, your mentor, *and* clever Loki."

Odin stood straight and tall. All doubt had long since vanished from the god's face. He lifted his chin proudly and stared down at them with his one eye and singular vision.

"I tricked you all."

"SO YOU TRICKED US," PRU SPAT. HER DETACHMENT WAS GONE. HER EYES burned with fury. "But you killed your son. *Your son!* And you're *proud* of it! *You're a monster!*"

"MY SON WAS ALREADY DEAD! He died the day I drank from the Well of Wisdom. I watched him die. I watched *everyone* die. Do you understand? *You're all already dead.*" Odin snorted with contempt. "You just don't know it yet."

"We'll stop you," ABE said. He wondered if the words sounded as clichéd and hollow to the others as they did to him.

"Will you?" Odin laughed. "And how will you do that?"

"We'll tell Thor," Pru said. "And the other gods."

"They would not believe you. Besides, you will not get the chance. The gods will no more return to Midgard. Even my errant son, Thor, has learned his place. And you have no means to get to Asgard. Your mentor is dead. So is the rodent you called friend."

"Ratatosk is dead?" Pru took a wounded step back.

"Garm's most recent prey."

"All these deaths," ABE said, trying not to imagine poor Ratatosk in Garm's jaws. "Pru's right. You *are* a monster."

"Worse," Pru said. "You're a coward!"

Odin swung his walking stick through the air. Midswing, it became a vicious-looking spear, its blade glinting in the sun. It hung in the air between them.

"I could kill you. Sometimes I do, you know." Odin's eye took on a faraway look. "But I think I will not be so kind. I will leave you with the greatest curse I know. You will live on with your knowledge of what is to come. Let us see if you bear that burden better than I."

Odin turned his back on them. He whispered something ABE didn't understand, and a curtain of light appeared before him—Bifrost, the rainbow bridge that led to Asgard.

"Your part in this is done, children. Be grateful that your lives have been so touched by greatness. Farewell."

Odin stepped into the light and vanished.

ABE dropped to his knees. "What have I done? I condemned Loki. He was innocent."

Pru spun to face the ocean and hugged her arms to her chest. Her shoulders shook.

"We have to do something," he said. "Pru?"

She remained silent.

"Pru!"

"What can we do, ABE?" Her face was wet with tears when she turned to look at him. "Mister Fox is dead. Ratatosk is dead. Odin's right. We lost."

"We could try . . ."

"*Try what?* He's seen the future, ABE. He's seen *every* future! He'd know everything we did before we did it. He's unstoppable."

He didn't want her to be right. He didn't want to be Odin's pawn. Mister Fox had said nothing was worse than letting someone else choose your role for you. But Odin had chosen everyone's roles—and he'd gotten away with it.

Now Ratatosk and Mister Fox were dead and gone forever, and nothing, *nothing* could ever change that.

Or so he thought.

"No, no, no!" a high-pitched voice behind him said.

ABE rose and spun around in one fluid motion, not quite daring to believe his ears. A small, rough-looking gray squirrel with a notch in his left ear sat on the ground a few feet away.

"Ratatosk!" Pru cried. She ran forward as the squirrel bounded to her. She skidded to her knees and Ratatosk jumped into her lap. "But . . . how? Odin said you were dead!"

"Almost was, yes! Might have been! Garm had me in his teeth. Everything went black. Then . . . I opened my eyes in the Queen of the Dead's palace. The queen gave me safe passage from Niflheim! Strange, yes? Bewildering! Incomprehensible!"

"A kindness," ABE whispered, remembering his dream and the queen's words. "She said she would return something we'd lost."

"What?" Pru said, glancing up at him.

"It's not important. I'll explain later. What matters now is that Ratatosk's back! But what I don't get is how."

"Who cares? It doesn't matter. All that matters is that he *is* back. He's not dead." Pru scratched Ratatosk's nose and the squirrel chittered happily.

ABE shook his head, though Pru wasn't paying any attention to him.

It did matter. Didn't it?

Odin could see the future. He should have known that Ratatosk would come back. Unless . . . What if he could see the future . . . but he wasn't *looking*?

"Pru, do you remember when Odin told us the story of how the Eye of Odin came to be? He said that when he went to the Well of Wisdom, he went in a disguise and the guardian didn't recognize him."

"I remember." Pru didn't look up. She merely shifted her attention from Ratatosk's nose to scratching behind his ear. "So what?"

"You joked that the guardian wasn't very good at his job if he was so easily fooled. I remember because Odin got defensive. He said the guardian was farseeing. He told *us* to try looking out at a beach sometime and seeing every grain of sand at once."

"So?"

"Well, maybe Odin got defensive because he has the same problem the guardian did. Odin saw so many futures. He's farseeing. But maybe he can't see every grain of sand at once. Maybe he can't keep all those futures straight in his head." ABE spoke quickly, unable to contain his excitement. "Don't you see? Ratatosk is alive. That means Odin can be wrong! He doesn't know everything."

Pru stopped scratching Ratatosk's head and chewed her lip. "Maybe . . ." she agreed.

Ratatosk cleared his throat and nudged Pru's hand. She smiled at the squirrel and stood, placing Ratatosk on her shoulder.

"Maybe you're right, ABE. And maybe it's important. But I don't want to think about it right now. Everything went so wrong. And Mister Fox . . . Look,

I'm tired. I just want to be glad Ratatosk is alive. I'm going to take him home and let him rest. Okay?"

ABE nodded. This wasn't the time to push Pru. She'd be ready to talk soon enough. Then he could explain why he was so excited. It could wait until tomorrow.

Tomorrow. It was such a simple word. But, really, it was the most important word.

We all hope for more time.

That's what Alva had said when she'd defended the gods and their failure to act on the day of Baldur's death. But the gods weren't the only ones guilty of taking tomorrow for granted. ABE had done it, too.

It had been the worst part about learning that Ragnarok was coming. Ragnarok meant an end to all tomorrows. But if Odin could be wrong about Ratatosk, maybe he could be wrong about Ragnarok, too.

Maybe. *Possibly.* It wasn't certain.

But that was the point, wasn't it?

ABE didn't know what would happen next. So many questions remained. Everything seemed so uncertain. But somehow, that uncertainty suddenly felt like a victory. Odin had wanted them to believe that he had all the answers, that the future was sure and set. That wasn't true. Uncertainty survived—and with it the magic of possibility.

They'd lost so much. Now, though, ABE felt like they had won back tomorrow.

ABE closed his eyes and pictured Mister Fox, knowing he'd never see the detective again, except perhaps as a ghost in the looking glass. He felt a rush of sorrow, but he also felt gratitude and a deeper appreciation for the detective as—for the first time—he truly understood why Mister Fox had been such a champion of uncertainty.

Sometimes it really was okay not to know.

And, with that realization, ABE discovered the answer to another question, one he had nearly forgotten. He had one last battle to fight that day.

ABE FOUND HIS DAD TINKERING WITH THE LAWN MOWER WHEN HE RETURNED home.

"What happened?" ABE asked.

"The front wheel cracked," his dad said. "Must have been a rock or something. I pulled this replacement off the old mower in the shed. It's not a perfect fit, but I think it will do for now. Hand me that wrench?"

"Sure." ABE crouched down beside his dad. "Can we talk for a minute?"

"You bet." His dad gave a final twist to the bolt that secured the wheel, then settled back against the front step. "What's up?"

"I kind of wanted to talk to you about Danny. He's that kid who was on the bike the other day."

"I remember. What's wrong? Is he still giving you a hard time?"

"No. Well, actually, yeah. But that doesn't matter."

"It *does* matter, ABE. You can't just let people—"

"No, Dad, wait, okay? Just listen."

His dad opened his mouth, then closed it without saying a word. He nodded.

"Danny can be a jerk. But he's not the problem."

"He's not? Who is, then? Who's giving you a hard time?"

"That's just it. *You* are, Dad."

"Me?"

"Yeah. I mean, I know you're trying to help. I do. I know you don't like the idea that Danny is picking on me. But it's like I said. Danny can be a jerk. So why should I care what a jerk thinks of me? And the thing is, I don't. I do care what *you* think of me, though."

"ABE, you're my son. I love you."

"I know. But . . . but I want you to understand me, too. I heard you tell Mom that I don't stand up for myself."

"Oh, hey, ABE, I'm sorry." His dad blushed. "I didn't mean for you to hear that."

"No. It's okay. See, I've been thinking about it and you're right. I don't stand up for myself a lot. For a while, I wondered if it was because I was scared. But you know what, Dad? I'm not. I mean, I do get scared, obviously. But I don't let that stop me. So I kept thinking about why I don't stand up for myself as much as I stand up for my friends."

"Oh? And did you come up with anything?"

"Yeah. Yeah, actually, I did. I think the reason I don't stand up for myself is because I'm still figuring *me* out. I mean, how do you stand up for yourself if you don't really know who you are yet? I'm still working on that. But that's okay. I mean, it's okay with me anyway. I've known a lot of people lately who have had other people tell them who they should be, or how they should act. That hasn't really worked too well for anyone."

ABE fell silent.

"I'll tell you this, ABE," his dad said. "Pru's mom got one thing right, that's for sure."

Were they talking about Pru now? ABE's shoulders sagged.

"You are one smart kid."

"Oh!" ABE smiled. "Ah, thanks."

"You're welcome." His dad grabbed a rag and began to wipe some grease from his hand. "So listen. I know you and Pru like to go hiking. I did a lot of hiking in college. I learned a few things about following trails and wilderness survival. I was thinking maybe this weekend you and I could go out. If you'd like that, I mean."

"Really? Yeah! I think that would be great."

"Great." His dad stood. "I'm going to head in and wash up. You should probably get started on homework. After all, tomorrow is another day."

ABE stood, too.

"Yeah," he said, smiling. "Yeah, it really is."

ACKNOWLEDGMENTS

I have to start by thanking the fantastic group at Algonquin Young Readers: my editors, Elise Howard and Krestyna Lypen; the amazing group of marketers and publicists I worked with, including Brooke Csuka, Eileen Lawrence, and Trevor Ingerson; and my copy editors, Robin Cruise and Brunson Hoole. Their knowledge of and delight in children's literature, and their passion for getting books in the hands of young readers, was inspiring every step along the way.

I'd also like to thank Tarana Akhmedova, Andrea Lanoux, and Irina Shchemeleva for their help with the Russian terms in the book. ABE and Pru would still be wandering around in the dark without their help (and so would I).

Finally, I'd like to thank my critique group—Jane LeGrow (who also plays the part of my wife), Frances Kelley Prescott, Joan Domin, and Karen Lindeborg—for their support. I would also like to thank (belatedly) Sara Neilson, who was a reader for book 1 that I failed to thank (despite being thankful!).

And, of course, I'm grateful to everyone who has read (and hopefully enjoyed!) the Unbelievable FIB books. You are all Fibbers of the highest caliber.